Our Little Viking Cousin of Long Ago

This edition published 2026
by Living Book Press
Copyright © Living Book Press, 2026

ISBN: 978-1-76183-128-7 (hardcover)
        978-1-76183-127-0 (softcover)

First published in 1916.

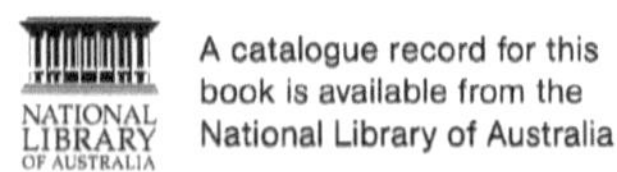
A catalogue record for this book is available from the National Library of Australia

Our Little Viking Cousin of Long Ago

by

Charles H. L. Johnson

BIARNE HERJULFSON

Contents

Hark to the story of Vinland,
        Vinland of grapes and wine,
Which Leif the Lucky discovered,
        —the land of hemlock and pine.
He sailed o'er the dark, blue ocean,
        with warriors thirty or more,
And planted his flag, with a cross and a shaft,
        on the beauteous, curving shore.
Huzzah, then, for Leif the Lucky!
        A hero may ever he be,
For his feet first trod on America's sod,
        in the year one thousand A. D.

PREFACE

The story of Biarne is laid at the time when the first venturesome seafarers crossed the Atlantic to explore the new and wonderful country of America. Although it is generally believed that Columbus discovered America, in 1492, the old Norse sagas give very conclusive evidence that the Vikings from Norway and Iceland were the first Europeans to set foot on the shores of the New World.

In the year 1000 A. D., Leif Ericson, known as Leif Lucky, a son of Eric the Red—the discoverer of Greenland—made a voyage from Greenland to the coast of New England. He was a hardy mariner, who feared no perils of land and sea. As an old Norse ballad says:

> He scorns to rest 'neath the smoky rafter,
> He plows with his boat the stormy deep;
> The billows boil, and the storm howls after,
> But the tempest is only a thing of laughter,
> The sea-king loves it better than sleep!

With thirty-five strong and adventuresome followers, he first cruised along the coast of Nova Scotia; then he sailed southward and went ashore at a place where a river flowed out from a lake into the sea. Here the ship was anchored; the men transported the luggage from the hold and built dwellings. They erected large buildings, and remained during the winter, and fared well upon the salmon with which the river abounded. In the spring they loaded their vessel with timber and set sail for Greenland. All of their friends were glad to see them again and eagerly heard tales of their good fortune. Two years later, Thorwald Ericson—Leif's brother—made a similar journey. If this story gives you, my dear boys and girls, a clear idea of the experiences and tribulations of these stalwart adventurers, the purpose of the author will have been fulfilled.

CHARLES H. L. JOHNSTON

CHAPTER I
The Christening

Joy reigned at the house of Biarne Herjulfson, for a little son had been born to that bold and hardy Norseman. At his great house, or boer, as it was called, all the retainers, maids-of-waiting, and fighting men went about with smiles upon their faces, and whispered to one another:

"The Nornir have left a message in the chimney that they will be with us to-morrow evening, and they said that the little one will have an adventurous life and will be a credit to our master."

"Thor, himself, who is the foremost of the gods, could not have had a more lusty voice when he was a stripling," spoke one of the serving men. "In truth, my good friends, I believe that the youthful heir to our house will be a great singer some day." Then all laughed with good humor, for there was a feast in store for them in commemoration of the joyful event.

It was believed by Norsemen that the future life of every child was shaped at its birth by the Fates, or Nornir, who seemed to have control of the gods themselves. There were three of these: Urd, the past; Verdandi, the present; and Skuld, the future; who lived at the foot of Urd's well, situated at the bottom of a large ash-tree, whose roots they watered with their wisdom and experience of the past, and where they spun the threads of fate at the birth of every child.

So, when the word was passed around that the Nornir had left a message in the chimney, that the new-born would have a great career, even Biarne Herjulfson, the rough, old father, smiled and chuckled with glee.

Next morning all the family and servants gathered in the great hall to witness the christening of the little son of the house. He was placed upon the floor and was left there for some time without being touched by any one. Then an old retainer, called Gormanud, walked forward, picked up the little Norseman, and placed him in the arms of his father, who held out his cloak so that it covered the body of his new born heir.

It was a custom of the Norsemen to look at a child two days after he was born and decide whether he should be placed outside upon the ground and left to die, or should be allowed to live. This was as the old Spartans used to do and was certainly a brutal custom, although these wild people seemed to think nothing of it. So, after old Biarne Herjulfson had received the child in his arms, he looked at it very carefully, so as to decide, from its appearance, whether its fortunes would be good or bad, and whether it would or would not be a great sea rover.

"Thou wilt be a bold and hardy warrior," said Biarne Herjulfson. "Thou wilt be a brave adventurer and wilt see great hardships and perils upon the sea."

He then walked to a large bowl in which was some water,

dipped in his hand, and sprinkled it over the body of the young Norseman, who was very quiet, and was gazing about him with wide, staring eyes. This was a religious rite called the Ausa Vatni.

Now it was time to give a name to the young Norseman; a custom which was called nafnfesti, or name-fastening. Consequently, an uncle of the child, called Thrudvangar, walked up to him, and, laying his hand upon the baby's head, said: "Little one, I christen thee Biarne, the second. I also give thee a sword, a helmet, a cuirass, and a spear, hoping that you will find good use for them in your life. I also present thee with a gold ring, which I trust that you will wear when your hand is of sufficient size to fill it. May you lead a brave and noble life; may you be a credit to your noble father, your good mother, and to all your family."

At this all of the servants and guests cried out:

"Hail! valorous Biarne!"

Large casks of ale had been rolled into the great Sal, or hall, in which this interesting event had taken place, and, after these were opened, great goblets of horn were dipped into them and were handed around among the guests. Two men with strange-looking fiddles, called gigja, came into the room, and also a harper with snowy-white hair, and a harp of gold. The sweet strains of music now arose above the hum of the voices of the guests, and all laughed loudly as the little Norseman—still in the folds of the cloak upon his father's arm—cried out with loud and vociferous tones.

But what was this?

Suddenly a hush fell upon all the guests assembled; the music ceased; and even the wails of young Biarne were stilled. At the far end of the room a strange figure was seen approaching. Clad in a long, black cloak was a woman with flowing gray hair, a thin, cadaverous face, and a large helmet upon her head, from which two great eagle wings extended into the air.

"It is one of the Nornir," whispered a lady-in-waiting. "It is Urd, the past!"

"No," whispered another. "It is Verdandi, the present!"

But the strange visitor looked neither to the right nor to the left. Stalking onward, she walked to where the long-bearded father was holding his little son in his arms, and, raising a thin arm above him, in a sort of benediction, she said, in deep, sonorous tones:

"Youth: Thy fate will be an auspicious one. Thou wilt wax strong and brave, and thou wilt go to far countries and wilt discover a land teeming with wild grapes. Thou wilt be a credit to thy parents and to thy country. But I, Skuld, do tell thee one thing which thou must remember: do not trust to one who passeth as thy friend, but who is not really such. Do not put your faith in a red-bearded man with a scar upon his forehead. I, Skuld, give you my blessing."

Suddenly, as if by magic, the strange figure disappeared. All looked aghast, for the apparition had vanished into the air.

'I, SKULD, GIVE YOU MY BLESSING.'

CHAPTER II
The Training of a Young Viking

"Come, little one, it is time for your exercise!"

The man who spoke was a large, bearded Norseman, who held a long spear in one hand and, in the other, a very small spear, which a boy could handle without much difficulty.

"I will be ready in a moment," said young Biarne,—now grown to be a youth of ten years of age.

It was the custom among the Norsemen to have their children educated for their future duties of life, at the home of some distinguished friend. When a child was received by a Norseman, his foster parent was bound to treat him with the same love and kindness as he would his own child. The child was brought to his new home by his own parent, who placed him upon the knees of his foster-father. The boy was then called the Knesetningr, or the Knee-seated one. This custom was called Knesetia, or Kneeseating,

Young Biarne had been brought to fierce, old Thorwald Knutsen, who was a great warrior and had been in many a battle on the ocean. He lived in a big house, about five miles from the house of Blame's father, and had a large ship of his own which lay in the bay, or fiord, before his residence, and which was rowed by one hundred men. Just now he was living at home, and was attending to the duties of his farm, but every year he went upon a voyage to the southward and came back with much treasure and many stories of fierce adventure with the Picts, the Scots, and other tribes of men who lived in Britain, and the other lands which lay near the wild North Sea.

It was the duty of every teacher to endeavor to make his pupil as strong as he could. Consequently, a boy was taught to ride, to swim, to travel over the deep snow on snowshoes, and how to use the sword and javelin.

Young Biarne followed his teacher out into the garden where a huge target had been hung upon a tree. Then Thorwald made him stand about ten feet away from it, take the javelin in his hand, and throw it at a bull's eye marked in the center.

"You are doing well," said Thorwald, after Biarne had made ten or twelve throws and had twice struck the bull's eye. "Now we will have an hour or two at walking with the dogs."

The Vikings all kept hawks for chasing birds, and also hounds for hunting. They had grey-hounds for running down small game, and also huge, shaggy wolf and bear-hounds for use in the deep forests. Thorwald had a kennel of dogs and he went down to let them out. But, before he did so, he walked up to the house and called out: "Eric! Eric! Come and join us in a hunt with the dogs."

A cry went up from inside: "All right, I am coming!" and soon a boy of the same age as Biarne, with pink cheeks and golden hair, came running down the graveled path which led from the great house.

Eric Grimolfson had also been sent to school under Thorwald, and his father lived not very far away. He was very fond of Biarne, and although they had only been together for a year, they were great companions.

Now the kennel door was opened, and the dogs, eight in all, bounded into the open. In a very few moments they reached the edge of the deep woods which surrounded the mansion house. No sooner had the dogs entered the edge of the forest than one of them set up a deep baying and howling, showing that he had smelled something.

In a moment all the dogs had started off upon a hot scent. They were soon out of sight, and almost out of hearing, although the boys tried their best to keep up with them.

After a short time, a deep baying in the woods showed that the dogs had stopped running. Thorwald cried out:

"Hurry up, boys, hurry. We must see what they have been after!"

Thorwald wore a big sword and had a javelin in his hand, while both Eric and Biarne were armed with short spears. , As they pressed onward they heard a great commotion in the woods, and, coming up with the dogs, saw that they had surrounded a huge, gray wolf, which showed its fangs, snarled evilly, and snapped at them when they approached.

"My, what a big fellow," said Eric. believe that he could kill any dog that attempted to seize him."

"I'll fix Mister Wolf," said Thorwald, as he walked up to within striking distance of the animal. Taking his javelin in his right hand, he hurled it at the beast with all of his might. The sharp point penetrated the animal's side, and, as he turned to bite at the shaft, the dogs were upon him with a rush.

"Good!" shouted Eric. "Now they will finish off Mister Wolf."

It was as he said. The odds were too great against the big, gray fellow, and in a few moments he was lying dead upon the moss of the forest, while the dogs savagely growled above his shaggy body.

"Now that you have seen a hunt," said Thorwald to the boys, "I will show you how to call off the dogs."

Putting a ram's horn to his lips, he blew a sharp blast, and started to walk away into the forest. The boys followed, and, after Thorwald had cried out right lustily: "High-on! High-on!" the dogs left their quarry and followed after.

"Now, boys, it is time for more gentle exercise," said Thorwald. "We will go to the house and will have some lessons upon the harp."

Although the young Vikings were taught how to be warriors and huntsmen, they were also taught to work in wood and metal, and how to play on the harp. To be a good harpist was considered to be the duty of every well-born Norwegian.

They soon reached the great house, called the Holl, and the dogs were put back into the kennels. Thorwald then led the boys into a long room, at the end of which was a large fireplace, and which was carpeted with heavy rugs. Several harps were here, and, taking his position before one, Thorwald gave a harp to each of the boys. Soon they were busily learning the music to a famous Norse saga, or song.

It was soon luncheon time. The music room was left behind and the boys went into the dining room, a low chamber hung with shields, with spears, and with the skins of bears, of wolves, of otter, mink, and foxes. Here they were cheerfully greeted by Thorwald's wife, Enid, and his two daughters, Rodny and Thorhilda, who spread a hearty meal before them.

Thorwald's wife was dressed in a long gown, or kirtle, which was made very wide with a train, and had big sleeves reaching to the wrists. It was fastened around the waist with a belt made of silver, from which a bag was suspended for keeping keys, rings, and ornaments. Over the kirtle was worn a bloeja, a kind of apron, with a fringe at the bottom.

After luncheon was over, the boys were told that they were to go riding. Three fine steeds were brought around to the door; Thorwald had soon mounted; the boys clambered upon the backs of their own horses, and soon all were off for a gallop into the country. When they returned, both Eric and Biarne were quite willing to remain quietly in the house, until bed time.

Thus were young Vikings trained. It was an athletic life, and, under such teaching, they were expected to develop into strong and hardy men.

CHAPTER III

Some Lessons in Viking Beliefs

No sooner had the bright beams of the sun penetrated the room in which Eric and Biarne were sleeping upon some bear skins, than both boys leaped to their feet and began to splash into their faces some water from a big stone jug which was in a corner of the chamber. Breakfast was soon over, and then Thorwald told the boys that a famous Skald, or poet, named Lothair, was coming that morning to instruct them in the Norse religion and also to recite some of the sagas or songs of the Vikings.

The boys were delighted to hear this, and when a tall man with a long, brown beard, came into the house, they ran to him and eagerly asked if he were Lothair.

"Yes, I am Lothair the Skald," said he, laughing. "And I have brought my harp with me so that I can sing to you boys after I have finished telling you about the Valkyrias."

"Who are they?" asked both of the boys, almost with the same breath.

Lothair seated himself in a big chair, after saying "good morning "to Thorwald, and began to speak:

"My boys," said he, "you must know that away up in

the heavens live the gods who watch over all of us. Thor is the foremost of them all, and he lives at Thrudvangar, 'The Plains of Strength,' in a hall of five hundred and forty rooms, called Bilskirnir.

"Each of us is watched over by a guardian spirit. Each of you boys has a guardian spirit who, though unseen, is always near you, and whose hand you can clasp in right good fellowship, although he is not visible to you."

"That is nice," said Eric. "I hope that I can see my guardian spirit some day. Some day when he is off his guard and needs company."

Lothair laughed.

"I am afraid that you will never see him," he answered. "But, when you are older and go into battle, I am sure that you will see some strange maidens near you. These are sent from Valhalla, the home of the gods, to determine the fate of battle, and they are called the Valkyrias. They can ride through the air, and also over the sea. Sometimes they ride upon the shafts of lightning, which are rays of sunshine coming from the face of the gods. Often they ride upon fiery steeds, clad in glittering armor, and they bear with them long spears, sharpened either for victory, or for death.

"At first, my boys, there were only six Valkyrias; but, as the years passed onward, there were nine. Once, indeed, twenty-seven of them were seen on a battle field; for an old poet has sung:

> "There were three times nine maidens,
> But one rode foremost
> A white maiden under a helmet;
> Their horses tremble,
> From their manes fell
> Dew into the deep dales,
> And hail on the lofty woods."

"Although these maidens nearly always live in the Heavens, at times they come to dwell upon the earth; and, upon one of these occasions, they were discovered by three royal princes.

"These princes were sons of one of the Kings of Sweden and used to spend much of their time running about upon snowshoes, for there was much snow in their country. They also hunted wild beasts, and killed many a large wolf and shaggy bear.

"One day the three young men came to a lake hidden deep in the forest, and they liked the place so much that they tarried there and built a house, where they lived for some time. Going down to the edge of the lake, one early morning, they beheld three beautiful women, who were spinning flax. The princes knew that they were Valkyrias, for nearby lay the swan-skins in which Valkyrias usually disguised themselves. It could be plainly seen that they had been caught unawares.

"The three brothers spoke gracefully and courteously to them and asked the Valkyrias to go home with them. The maidens consented, and lived seven years with the young men. But they were not happy; for, hearing afar the sound of battle, they were restless. One day they disappeared, never to return. In vain the princes sought for them. The sisters were soon amidst the din and carnage of war, and the brothers never saw them again!"

"What a nice story," Eric interrupted. "And do you think that we will see these sisters when we are men and can use sword and javelin in battle?"

Lothair laughed with great good humor.

"I've no doubt that you will, my son," he replied; "for the Valkyrias always hover over a battle-field, and look after those who are in trouble and distress.

"But never forget that only the valorous, and those who have done great deeds, shall be welcomed in Valhalla, 'The Hall of the Slain.' It has five hundred and forty doors, and each door is so wide that eight hundred warriors can pass through it at the same moment.

"Death should have no terror for you, for it is good to be welcomed to the glad halls of Valhalla; to sit down to feast at the festive board; and to welcome the brave in the halls of the gods. Death you shall not fear; but shame you must always dread, and this can only come to you if you flee before the foe. The greatest thing that a Viking can do is to win fame,—fame that will live in the sagas of the nation and will be handed down from generation to generation."

Both of the boys listened to him with the greatest attention. Already they had determined to stick manfully to their lessons so as to become strong men and noble warriors.

"Now, boys," Lothair continued, "I will tell you the story

of Bjorn, a son of one of the Kings of Norway. Bjorn's own mother had died when he was a baby, and he had a stepmother who did not love him. Therefore, one day, she struck him with a bearskin glove, saying, as she did so, 'Thou shalt become a fierce bear, and thou shalt eat no food save thy father's cattle. So much cattle shalt thou kill that all men shall hear of it, and never shalt thou escape from this spell.'

"As she finished speaking, a great bear ran out of the courtyard, and Bjorn was never seen or heard of again.

"The King, who was very fond of his son, sought for him throughout the realm, but it was in vain. No signs of him were ever seen. But, from the day that Bjorn vanished, it is said that a fierce, gray bear was often to be seen prowling around among the cattle of the King, until the numbers grew less and less.

"So you see, boys," said Lothair, "that you can change your form into that of an animal. And, if you but eat the flesh and drink the blood of some wild beast, you will become as strong and fierce as the animal of whose blood you have partaken."

"Then I shall drink wolf's blood," said Biarne. "But how is it that you are not fierce, Lothair, as you are a great huntsman?"

The Skald laughed with much good humor.

"My boys," said he, "I am a singer, and singers are not fierce, for their souls are softly tempered by the music which they play. Now, if you wish, I will sing to you to the music of my harp."

The boys sprawled out, full length, upon a big bearskin

rug, while Lothair took his harp and sang to them a song of the valorous deeds of the Vikings. Thus were they instructed in the history of their forefathers and were told of the great battles which had been fought both on land and upon the surging ocean.

CHAPTER IV
How Thor Lost His Hammer

The next morning dawned cold and blustery, with a chill wind blowing, so the boys were informed by Thorwald that they would not go out horseback riding, or to practice with the javelin; but would spend their time in playing upon the harp and learning about the gods and their life at Thrudvangar, "The Plains of Strength."

Lothair had spent the night with them, and, in the morning, told them that he had a story to tell them. They all went into the long room, and, after some huge logs had been heaped upon the fireplace, the boys lay down before it, while Lothair and Thorwald stretched themselves out in long chairs.

"Boys, as I have told you before," said Lothair, "Bilskirnir, the Palace of the great god Thor, King of all the gods, is built in his Kingdom of Thrudvangar, the realm that lies beyond the thunder clouds. It is the largest palace that has ever been roofed over for it has five hundred and forty halls beneath its silver dome, and it is so bright and so dazzling that when people on the earth catch a glimpse of it through the clouds, they blink their eyes and say that they have seen lightning. Thor spends most of his time there. When he is not away from home, fighting giants or attending assembly meetings, he is wandering around in the five hundred and forty halls, or sitting in a tremendous hall in the center of Bilskirnir. Around the walls he has benches placed for his followers; gleaming weapons hang there; great fires blaze upon the hearth of gold; while in the center, beneath a high, crystal dome, Thor, the Splendid One, has a high throne of glittering magnificence.

"Now, boys, Thor had a great hammer of which he was very proud. He called it The Crusher (Mjolnir) because nothing could withstand a blow from it when delivered by his arm. When he slept, it always lay near him, within easy reach of his hand. Some dwarfs had made this great weapon for him and he was very proud of it, I can assure you. When he struck a blow, all the heavens pealed with a clap of thunder, and way down below the people would gaze upward and would say: 'Thor has made a mighty blow with his hammer. Thor must again be angry.'

"One night Thor was sleeping in his palace, surrounded by his retainers, who had gone to rest on cushioned benches. Among his followers was one Loki—known as the Sly One—who was visiting him, and who sprawled at full length upon some cushions near the fire, glowing brightly in the great golden hearth. Thor had a red beard, and it was tossed up in the air as he leaned back in his high seat. His bushy brows had a frown upon them, for a bad dream was troubling his usually tranquil mind. Thor, in fact, had dreamed that his hammer had been stolen by Thrym, the Giant King who lived not far away in the heavens, and who was very jealous of Thor and his power.

"The god of all gods awoke with a start and sat up. He looked about him. He was safe in his own hall, and his retainers slept peacefully around him. He could hear their gentle snoring, as they dreamed away upon the cushioned benches. It seemed to be impossible that anything could have happened, yet he felt that something ill had befallen him, and, to make sure, he put out his hand and reached for his hammer, that weapon before which nothing could stand. Instantly Thor's red face grew ashen pale, for The Crusher had gone!

"The Strong One uttered such a wild yell that it was heard far down below upon the earth, and the Vikings thought that a thunder storm was brewing. Thor's beard quivered with righteous anger, and he leaned over to where Loki, the Sly One, was sleeping, and clutched him by the arm.

"'Awake, Loki!' said he, 'a terrible calamity has overtaken me. My good hammer, my trusty sledge hammer+ has been stolen what shall I do? I will now be powerless in warfare, and no longer can my peals of thunder ring out to warn the people on earth that I am alive and am god of all gods!'

"The Sly One jumped up, rubbed his eyes, and looked at Thor's troubled face. Loki was clever, so, after thinking the matter over for some time, he said:

"'I think that Thrym has stolen your hammer. But you must not go to him, for, like your red beard, you are of a fiery nature, and you would kill him ere you have learned whether he has your hammer or not. Therefore, let me visit Thrym. I will disguise myself in the feather-dress of Freyja, the lovely one. I will get news to you of your hammer. If possible, I will steal it myself.'

"Thor's face grew more calm and tranquil.

"'I will reward you greatly if you recover my hammer, Loki!' said he. 'I cannot be happy without it.'

"'Wait for me, Thor, god of all gods,' Loki replied. 'I will be sure to bring you good news.'

"The Sly One immediately went outside and harnessed up two goats to a silver chariot. 'I will go to the goddess Freyja's palace,' said he. 'I will borrow her dress of feathers, and, thus disguised, I will go to the land of the giants, and will find out whether or not Thor's hammer is there.'

"Loki soon arrived at Freyja's immense palace and, when he asked her for her dress, she gladly gave it to him. It was made of the white and brown plumage of falcons and fitted Loki's body like a glove.

"The Sly One then spread his wings and flew out of the window, on and on and on, until he arrived at Jotunheim, where the giants all lived. There Thrym had his home. Thrym was very, very large, and he was also very old. He had a long beard which glittered like frost and shone like molten silver. His hands and face were covered with short, glistening hairs. He was crafty and cruel, and, when Loki alighted before him, he apparently was expecting him, for he looked up with a wicked smile, and said:

"'Welcome, Sly One. Welcome, O Loki! How fares Thor, god of all gods? How fare the elves? How fares the beautiful Freyja? Why do you come alone to Jotunheim?'

"Loki looked sternly and fearlessly at him.

"'Ill fares the Mighty One. Ill fares the beautiful Freyja. Ill fare the elves,' said he. 'Thor has lost his hammer and I think that you have it. Have you not stolen Thor's hammer? And where have you concealed it?'

"Thrym grinned, even laughed derisively.

"'Yes, I have Thor's hammer,' said he. 'I have concealed it eight lengths beneath the ground. I intend to keep it until Freyja, the Beautiful One, becomes my bride. No man can have it unless Freyja becomes mine.'

"Loki burst out laughing. 'Think of it! Freyja the bride of such a horrible, old giant? Freyja—sweet, lovely Freyja—to become the wife of a wicked ugly monster!' His very soul revolted at such a thought, and he laughed long and loudly, while Thrym grinned, turned his back on him, and began to talk to his many white horses, with long manes and still longer tails, which he had all about him.

"Loki said again:

"'Is this the only answer that you give?

Remember that Thor is god of all gods, and that his vengeance is swift and sure. Demand not too much of Thor.'

"Thrym glowered savagely at him.

"'What do I care for Thor,' said he; ' I have his hammer. What can he do without it?'

"Loki saw that it was useless to talk with him further, so he spread his shining wings, leaped into the air, and flew back over the world to Thrudvangar, where Thor was eagerly waiting for him."

"And, now, boys, we will all have some luncheon," said Thorwald, at this point in the narrative, "and, when it is all over, Lothair will tell you how Thor regained his mighty hammer."

The boys jumped up, right merrily, and soon they were all feasting around the long, oaken table.

CHAPTER V
How Thor Regained His Lost Weapon

Luncheon was soon over. The boys were eager to hear the rest of the tale, so Lothair again seated himself in his oaken chair, and continued his narrative.

"Thor had been very anxious when Loki had flown away to visit Thrym, for he did not wholly trust the Sly One, and he was afraid that he would not return at all. So, when his feather-dress appeared at the doorway of Bilskirnir, he cried out, in a stern voice:

"'Well, well, Loki, have you succeeded in your errand? What have you learned about my hammer, pray? What has old Thrym been doing, eh? Hurry! Speak up! I am anxious to hear!'

"Loki looked fearlessly at the god of all gods.

"'Well, I have found out everything!' said he. 'Thrym, the King of the Giants, has your hammer. He will not return it unless first the beautiful Freyja becomes his bride. 'What think you of that?'

"Thor grew so angry that he fairly snorted, and his red beard stuck out in the air as if charged with electricity. He growled out his answer with such force that the heavens reverberated with thunder, and the people down on the earth looked fearfully into the air as flashes of lightning played above them.

"'Hah! What is this you tell me, Loki? Is it true that Thrym has sent me such a message? Is it to win the beautiful Freyja that he has made all this trouble? We will ride to see her without delay.'

"So the chariot drawn by his two goats was brought around before the palace. Thor and Loki jumped inside, and soon were speeding through the air to visit the beautiful Freyja, whom they found sitting upon her throne and playing with her wonderful necklace, whose beads sparkled and flashed like drops of water upon which the sun is shining.

"'I am delighted to see you, Thor,' said she, as the god of all gods drew up before the door. Loki flew up to her and dropped at her feet the feather dress which he had borrowed.

"'Thrym has stolen my hammer, Beautiful One,' said Thor. 'He refuses to bring it back until you become his bride. What think you of that, Freyja?'

"The Lovely One grew scarlet with rage, and her hand caught in her necklace and broke it into a thousand little sparkling globules. She cried out, angrily:

"'What? Become the bride of that horrible old monster? Never! Never! I say, never!'

"Thor looked at her with great surprise, for he considered the hammer of such importance that he thought that any one would do anything for him in order to regain it.

"'Well, if I do not get my hammer back, you will probably be captured by Thrym and his giants, for, if they should invade the sky, I would have nothing to fight them with. Hence you would be carried away by force.'

"Freyja said nothing, but looked sorrowfully at both him and Loki, who was whistling a tune, and was nervously tapping his foot upon the palace floor.

"Thor continued as before:

"'I do not see why you do not marry Thrym. He has got great riches. He has twenty milk-white steeds. He has a herd of black oxen and an hundred cows with golden horns.'

"But Freyja had no wish to become the bride of the terrible giant. She stamped her foot and ran out of the hall and slammed the door in the face of the two visitors.

"Thor hung his head dejectedly and ran his hands over his beard.

"'Loki,' said he, at length, 'we will see what my kinsmen have to say about this. Come on! We will visit all the gods and will confer with them.'

"Jumping again into the chariot, the two goats were urged onward, and Thor and Loki sped away into the air, while Thor growled so savagely, in anger, that the people down on the earth looked above, saying: 'Hark! What a terrible thunder shower is brewing!'

"Thor drove to nearly every palace in the sky, and invited all the gods to a conference with him. Soon all were gathered together on the plains of Ida. There was Odin, the All Wise

Ruler; Balder, the Bright; Heimdal, the White One; Tyr; Broge; and Vale. They had a long consultation over what was to be done so that Thor could regain his hammer. At last Heimdal, the White One, spoke loudly, and said:

"'It is my advice that we play a trick upon the King of these giants by making him believe that we have done as he asked Loki to do. I suggest that we dress Thor in bridal robes and send him to see Thrym. He can play that he is the beautiful Freyja, can find out where his hammer is hid, and, when Thrym is not looking, he can seize it and can get away.'

"'Good! Good!' said all, and they laughed heartily.

"But Thor did not think so well of it. For was he not the strongest man in the Heavens? And was he not the god of all gods? Imagine him, Thor, dressed up as a beautiful woman with his long, red beard hidden by a kerchief. Thor scowled with anger.

"Loki, however, was anxious to have this done.

"'You should do this, Thor,' said he, 'else the giants will come and take your palace away from you, as you have no hammer to defend yourself with.'

"Thor knew that this was true, so he could do nothing but submit when they brought Freyja's jewels, her long robes, and her veil, and proceeded to dress him up like a woman.

They put on a girdle and hung a bunch of jingling keys from his waist in order to show that he was a good house-keeper. They braided his red hair into two long braids, and put a long stick in his right hand. Then they put on a cap with a long veil attached, so that no one could see his red beard. And, in spite of the fact that he raged and fumed at all of this, every one laughed at him. All the heavens echoed with the laughter of the gods, so that those below thought that many thunder squalls were brewing. And Thor scowled and fumed, but he knew that he must subject himself to all of this, if he were ever to regain his lost hammer. Loki then dressed himself as a servant maid, and, when all was ready, the chariot was brought up, and away went Thor and Loki to the palace of Jotunheim.

"Thrym heard them coming when they were a long way off and, as he was sure that the beautiful Freyja was approaching, he cried out to his followers: 'Arise, giants, and spread embroidered cloths over the benches. Fill the golden goblets with sparkling wine, for Freyja is coming to be my bride.'

"The golden chariot was drawn by the Goat-That-Gnashes-His-Teeth and the Goat-That-Flashes-His-Teeth, and they struck out fiery sparks from their golden-shod hoofs as they pranced along above the clouds. Just as twilight fell the chariot thundered into the courtyard, and, as Thor had on Freyja's jewels, her robes, and her headdress, Thrym thought that it was certainly she. He consequently took her hand, led her to a seat, and smiling exultantly, sang out:

"'Much wealth have I! Many gifts have I!

Freyja, the Beautiful One, is all that I lack!'

"'Bring in much food!' he shouted. 'Every one must join me in my wedding feast!'

"All the giants seated themselves around a long table, and the feasting began. Thor fell to with a will, although he was careful to open only a small space in his veil so that he could swallow his food. He was very hungry; so hungry, in fact, that he forgot that he was a dainty lady. What do you think? He ate up seven whole salmon, one whole side of an ox, a gallon of curds and honey, and washed it all down with three barrels of sweet and spicy mead, or ale. Loki kicked him under the table, saying:

"'Don't eat so much, Thor. You will give yourself away! Don't eat so much!'

"But Thor ate up another entire salmon.

"'Whew!' said Thrym. 'I never saw a bride eat so much before! I never saw a woman drink so much mead!'

"Thor heard what he said and began to get alarmed; for, if the giant should discover who he was, before he obtained possession of his hammer, he would kill him. He sat there silently looking before him, when Loki spoke, and said:

"'Freyja is very hungry, O Thrym, for has she not come eight days upon this journey? Freyja is thirsty, for eight days is a long time to travel.'

"Thrym began to look more complacent. 'Yes,' he answered. 'That is a long time to travel.'

"But now Thrym thought that he would like to implant a kiss upon Freyja's swan-like cheek. So, before Loki could stop him, he reached out with a great hairy hand and pulled at the bridal veil. He jerked it aside just far enough to see Thor's furious, little fiery eyes.

"Thrym sprang backwards, shouting out:

"'Why are Freyja's eyes so sharp? Fire is burning in the eyes of the Beautiful One!'

"But Loki, the Sly One, was again ready for the emergency.

"'Freyja has not slept for eight long nights,' said he. 'It took eight long days and eight long nights to come to Jotunheim.'

"'My, is that so,' said Thrym. 'I do not wonder that my beloved one is tired and red eyed.' He returned to his seat, but continued to look lovingly at his bride-to-be.

"But time wore on, and the moment arrived for the presentation of the bridal gifts. An old giantess, Thrym's sister, came up to where Thor was seated, and, bowing low before him, said:

"'Give me the golden rings from your hand, if you desire my friendship and my love.'

"Thor kept silent, for he knew that the moment he took the gloves from his hairy hands he would be discovered.

"But Thrym feared that his bride had been offended by the request, so he spoke up, and said:

"'Bring me Thor's great hammer, which I stole from him. Place it upon the maiden's lap, and wed us together in the name of Var.'

"How Thor did smile when his beady eyes fell upon his beloved hammer, as it was drawn out of its hiding-place and borne towards him. He sat there as stiff as a poker. There was danger if his disguise was discovered before his hand should grasp the hammer. Nearer, always nearer, the giant's attendants came with it. Nearer, always nearer, until, at last, they laid it on his knees!

"Thor's mighty fist closed upon the handle of his trusty weapon. He now feared no one in the heavens. He threw back his veil; he leaped to his feet. His red beard stood out straight on all sides. His fierce eyes blazed upon the assembled giants. His arm flew back to strike one of his mighty blows!

"'Cr-a-a-sh!' The thunder shook the halls of Jotunheim with a loud, reverberating peal, and Thrym fell dead at the feet of the god of all gods. 'Cr-a-a-sh!' and the old giantess lay dead beside her brother. Again and again the fearful hammer fell, until all the giants had been beaten to death, and lay like the trunks of fallen trees. Loki was laughing and dancing about in a frenzy of joy, for his strategy had been a complete success.

"Thus did Thor, the son of Odin, regain his mighty hammer. It was all due to a smart and crafty trick, and to the aid and assistance of Loki, the Sly One."

CHAPTER VI

A True Viking Must Be a Farmer
as Well as a Warrior

The boys clapped their hands, gleefully, when Lothair had finished his story.

"My," said Eric. "Wasn't Loki a crafty fellow, though?"

Thorwald laughed.

"But, boys," said he, "you must now continue your lessons, for, if you are to be true Vikings, you must learn not only to be warriors, but also to be farmers, builders of houses, and fishermen. An old Skald has sung:

> "'You must learn to tame oxen,
> And till the ground,
> To timber houses,
> And build barns,
> To make carts,
> And form plows.'

"All of our warriors, and even our mighty chieftains, must lay aside their weapons and work in the fields side by side with their thralls, or men, in sowing, reaping, and threshing. Even Kings must help their men cut the golden grain. All work is an honorable deed."

"We will be glad to work," said Biarne. "We wish to be true Vikings."

"You must learn how to thresh wheat," continued Thorwald. "If our crops fail there is great distress in the land."

"Have you heard the story of Helgi," interrupted Lothair, "and how he escaped from his enemies?"

"No, no, tell it to us," said both the boys.

"Once a man named Helgi disguised himself as a woman thrall in order to escape from his enemies," Lothair began. "In vain his enemies searched for him; Helgi was nowhere to be found. At length, as they looked for him far and wide, his enemies came to a barn in which was a hand mill for grinding corn. A tall, strongly built woman was turning the handle, but she worked very violently, so that the mill stones cracked and the barn was shattered to pieces, as fragments of the stone flew hither and thither.

"'Ah, ha!' said Helgi's enemies. 'This corn grinder is too vigorous to be a woman.'

"Then they pounced upon her, saying: 'More suited to these hands is the sword-hilt than the handle of the mill.'

"Helgi indeed it was. Helgi who had disguised himself as a female thrall. But—would you believe it—with the quick humor which, at times, steals over all of our people, Helgi's enemies forgot to punish him, as they laughed together over his disguise. 'Ha! Ha! Ha!' laughed they. 'His strength was too great for the disguise of a woman!'

"Now, come on, boys," said Thorwald. "We will go out

and will first plant some corn. Then you shall help me to start the building of a house."

The Norsemen built their own houses, for they were carpenters as well as warriors and farmers.

The boys went out into a field nearby, were given some oats, in sacks, and were soon busy in sowing it over the ground.

After they had done this for some time they were given some carpenter tools and were instructed by Thorwald in the methods of building a house.

Many of the houses of the Vikings had only one room. The side walls were long and low, with neither windows nor doors. The entrance was at the gable end, where a small door opened into a tiny vestibule. Through this one stepped into the large living-room, or hall.

The windows were merely open spaces between the beams which formed the roof of the house. There were wooden shutters outside.

A hole was left above the center of the room by which the smoke from the fire escaped. The Norsemen had no chimneys in their dwellings. The floor was made of clay, beaten hard; while the hearth was formed by placing several large, flat stones on the center of the clay floor. Here the fire blazed merrily away, while the smoke escaped through the hole in the roof. Benches, which were often used as beds, were fixed to the walls.

A few chests were sometimes provided, in which were

kept the household treasures, although many of the Vikings placed their jewels, their silver, and their gold in a large copper box, or a large horn; then, digging a hole in the earth, they would bury their treasure, marking the spot with a stone, or by some sign known only to themselves.

Thorwald dressed in gay colors, for the Norsemen loved bright clothing. His kirtle, or coat, of blue, was held together by a waist belt. Over the kirtle was flung a scarlet cloak, fastened at the shoulder with a buckle, which was of gold, studded with gems.

"Now, boys," said he, "you must work away at carpentry, so that you can build houses as well as the best of the Vikings. After awhile you will be noble warriors and great men."

Eric lay down his saw and his hammer.

"I am tired of this kind of work," said he to Biarne. "I'd rather have some adventure and some excitement in life. Oh, for another hunt!"

"Yes," answered Biarne. "Another hunt, or a fight. This life is too tame."

They were soon to have plenty of adventure.

CHAPTER VII

The Building of the Ship

"**S**teady boy, steady, thou wilt hurt thyself. Get thee from beneath these timbers."

The man who spoke was a hairy-bearded Viking who was clad in a workman's garb. He was directing the transportation of some stout beams from his work-shop to the shore, where the skeleton of a ship was lying. Many Norsemen were at work upon the vessel. It great curving sides and high prow showed it to be a typical Viking ship.

The boy stepped aside at this command and allowed the men who were carrying the beams to pass by. Then he walked up to the sides of the vessel in order to watch the progress of the building of the graceful hull. It was Biarne, who had wandered down to see what was going on. He was full of curiosity.

"Biarne, I want to speak to you!" came a voice at his shoulder.

Turning around, Biarne saw Eric, who was carrying some boards on his shoulder.

"What is it, Eric?" he asked. "I see that you are well laden."

"I want to speak to you after I deposit these boards at the ship."

"Very good, I shall be glad to hear what you have to say."

Eric went down to the water's edge, laid down the boards, and was soon back at the side of his friend.

"This vessel is being built for Leif Ericson, the Lucky," said he. "And it is whispered that he is to sail far to the west, where he expects to find a great and prosperous new country."

"Ah!" answered Biarne. "And what of that?"

"Would you not like to go with him, and have some adventure?" Blame's eyes opened wide.

"I had not thought of it. I am too young. How could I man an oar?"

"I am young, also. But I long to see a new country and to have adventures of my own."

Biarne looked solemn.

"That is all very nice; but how could we persuade one of Leif's followers to take us along?"

"That is easily evaded. We will stow away in the hold, and then we will see the wonders of the New World!"

Biarne began to smile. "Why, the idea is wonderful!" said he. "We will wait until the expedition is ready to sail, then we will hide in the bow. Before any one knows it, we will be out at sea and they cannot bring us home. Eric, I am with you!"

Linked arm in arm the two boys walked up the beach, laughing and jesting. They had in them the true, adventurous spirit of the Vikings.

But how was it that Leif the Lucky had knowledge of this land lying far to the west? And how was it that he had determined to go in search of adventures in a strange and unknown country?

The Vikings were bold and hardy adventurers, for the name Viking means "son of the bay," or "son of the ocean." They loved the sea and the bays, or fiords, which were upon the shores of Norway, of Denmark, and of Sweden.

These keen navigators sailed all over the northern seas and some of them settled in Iceland. More than a hundred years after this, a Norseman, named Eric the Red, was ordered to leave Iceland because he had killed another Viking in a sudden fit of passion. He had heard rumors of a western country, so he set out to find it. He and his companions found an island, settled there for a summer, and, because the green grass looked so beautiful, called the place Greenland. Soon more Norsemen came there and several settlements were made in this lonely country.

At this time there lived a man called Biarne Herjulfson—the very same name which little Biarne had; in fact, he was one of his ancestors. His father lived in Iceland, and the adventurous Viking wandered about for a long time before returning to his home to see his parent. When he arrived in Iceland he found that his father had gone to the new Greenland Colony with Eric the Red. So away to the west sailed the bold adventurer, searching for Greenland and his father. He steered by the sun and stars in true Viking fashion, and kept on and on, expecting any moment to come to the low lying shores of Greenland.

Suddenly the cry of "Land! Land!" was heard.

The captain looked eagerly before him, but there was nothing that looked like Greenland. This was a heavily wooded shore, with low hills in the background, and not a country rough and snowbound, as Greenland was supposed to be. He coasted along the shore, sailed into many of the coves and bays, and ran into some wonderfully deep harbors. It was really the coast of Nova Scotia and not Greenland.

"I have lost my way," said the venturesome mariner.

So, turning the bow of the ship towards the north, he sailed back until he reached the shores of Greenland. There he found his old father, just as he expected that he would do. But he was full of the tales of that new land which he had seen far to the west. He told them to all whom he met.

The story of these strange, wooded shores came to the ears of Leif Ericson, known as Leif the Lucky.

"I will go and explore the far western ocean," said he. "And I will build me a goodly ship in which to voyage thither."

But a goodly ship could not be built in Greenland, as the timber there was not big enough, nor had they sufficient men who were skilled in boat building. So Leif had sent over to Norway for a boat sufficiently large for this expedition.

That is how the hammers and the axes came to ring in the little cove, where Biarne and Eric watched the building of the vessel which was to transport this famous adventurer and his followers to the country of the unknown.

Eagerly the boys watched the building of this little bark. It did not look much like the ships of to-day. The bow and the stern were fashioned so as to rise high out of the water, and the middle of the vessel was low and had no deck. There was room for thirty rowers, who were to use oars twenty feet long. A single mast was in the forward part of the ship and it had but one sail, which could be taken down when not in use. The shields of the warriors were hung along the sides of this curious-looking craft. At the prow was a beautifully carved figure of a bear. In the stern was a firm deck, while in the forepart of the vessel were only loose planks, upon which the sailors stepped.

Day by day the work progressed, until finally the mast was shipped, the sail was bent upon the single spar which ran across the top of the mast, and the seams were caulked. The Viking ship was ready to be launched.

Now came a day when all the Vikings gathered upon the shore to see the vessel plow its way into the waves. Leif Ericson was there; tall, well formed, with ruddy face and reddish hair. Near by were Hekia, Vathildi, and Halfrida, his sisters; also Thorbiorn, the son of Halfrida; and Thoruna, mother of the little Biarne. Then there were many others; strong and athletic people of ruddy health, with the blue of the Baltic Sea reflected in their eyes. Hake and Hekia, cousins of Leif Ericson; Staumfroid, Thorhall and Ingveld, stout followers of the noble-hearted Leif. 'With cheerful faces and eager glances they watched the vessel as the pinning was knocked from under its sides, and with a great "swish "and a "splash "it plowed its way into the harbor.

"Hurrah!" cried Eric. "The good ship will soon be on its western journey."

"Hurrah!" whispered Biarne to him. "It will not be long, now, before we have an opportunity to go forth in search of adventure."

And all the people upon the shore gave a great shout as the graceful hull floated upon the waters of the little bay.

"Good luck to the good ship *Valhalla!*" cried all, and the cry was taken up by the gulls which wheeled and circled above, with much apparent interest and delight in the christening of the new vessel.

"Good luck to the good ship *Valhalla!*"

CHAPTER VIII
The Voyage to Vinland

"Hist, Biarne, are you ready?"

Biarne felt a tug at his shoulder. He sat up, yawned, and looked wonderingly around him, for he was in his own little bed in the house near the blue fiord, upon the waters of which floated the newly christened *Valhalla*.

"Is that you, Eric?"

"Yes. All is ready. Leif and his men are preparing to set sail this morning, and, if you and I are to go, we must hasten to stow ourselves away where they cannot see us."

"What time is it?"

"Near four o'clock in the morning and the cocks will soon be crowing."

Biarne leaped out of bed and hastily put on his clothes. He had a suit called a biafal, which consisted of a single garment, open at the sides, without arms, and fastened with a button and a strap. He seized a bag, which he had lying nearby, and in which he had placed a change of clothing, some warm outer garments to keep off the wind and the rain, and another pair of shoes. Then he was all ready to join the expedition.

Eric was older than Biarne, by a year, and Eric was filled

with the spirit of adventure. He led the way carefully to the beach, seated himself in a little boat, and pushed off towards the *Valhalla*, which could be dimly seen in the misty murk of dawn. Fortune favored the two adventurers. They found no sentinel on watch, and, clambering over the side, were soon looking for a place to hide themselves, so that they would be taken away without being discovered, until it was too late to make them return to their home.

"Here is where we will hide," whispered Eric, as he discovered a small opening between some large casks of fresh water. "See, there are some pieces of canvas that we can put over us, and then no one can possibly see us until we are far out at sea."

"Splendid!" said Biarne. "Splendid!" And, as a splashing of the water nearby showed that a boat was being rowed toward the ship, the boys quickly stowed themselves away in their hiding place.

They had not crouched there a very long time, before, with a great scraping and bustling, two men hauled themselves over the sides of the vessel and began to pile some boxes into the hold. One of them moved a box to a position immediately next to where the boys were hiding, but it did not disturb them in the slightest. They crouched down very close to the deck and said nothing. As luck would have it, they were not discovered.

A little later more boats put out to the *Valhalla* and other seafarers came on board. Leif Ericson, himself, climbed over the side, with a great roaring and singing, so that one would think that some minstrel were going to sea, and not a hardy Norse adventurer.

By daybreak all were ready to leave for the unknown West. The bow of the staunch ship *Valhalla* was turned towards the open sea, and, with a rousing cheer, the Vikings seized their long sweeps and dipped them into the blue water of the fiord. A few of the women had gathered on the beach, and these waved a fond adieu, as the high-sided, curiously shaped vessel plowed its way into the Atlantic.

Eric and Biarne crouched low behind the boxes and bales which hid them from the eyes of the Vikings, and, although their legs became very cramped, and they had strange, tingling sensations in them, they nevertheless managed to keep hidden from view.

"How long will we have to crouch down here?" whispered Eric, when the ship had traveled about a mile from the shore.

"We will remain hidden until we have been a day's journey from the land," said Biarne. "Then it will be impossible for Leif to send us back, when we show ourselves."

Eric smiled. "That's a fine idea," said he. "Biarne, you have a long head upon your shoulders."

The ship made good progress, for the wind was fresh, and the great sail bellied out with the steady drive of the breeze. The oarsmen at the sweeps were stout fellows, too, and they churned up the water of the ocean with their long oars. Leif the Lucky stood at the helm, with a great helmet, with two

ERIC AND BIARNE BECAME VERY CRAMPED
IN THEIR HIDING-PLACE.

eagle wings upon either side, on his head. A great, hairy coat of bearskin was thrown around his shoulders. To his right was his trusted friend and adviser, Thorbiorn; while nearby stood a Viking who had been with that first adventurer who had sailed near the coast of Nova Scotia, Staumfroid, the fearless one. Thorwald Ericson, Leif's cousin, was also of the party.

Eric and Biarne became very cramped in their hiding-place, and their muscles became very stiff and sore. But they held on for the space of a full day and a night. Then they crept out upon the deck to be greeted with loud laughter by those who were at the oars.

"Well! Well! Boys!" said one of the Vikings. "You're with us, sure, and I do not see how we are going to get rid of you; but I doubt if you can stand the hardships of the voyage."

"Oh, yes, we can," cried Biarne. "We, too, are Vikings!"

Just then Leif Ericson, himself, walked up.

"Well spoken, stripling," said he. "I see that you have the spirit of a real Viking in you. Right welcome are you both, and I know that youths of your caliber will be able to share the perils and the hardships of our expedition."

So saying, he gripped each by the hand, and they knew that they had before them a true hero, a man of dauntless daring and undefatigable purpose.

The boys were soon made to feel thoroughly at home. Instead of being badly treated by the Vikings they were patted on the back, were given a hearty meal, and were told that the older men were glad to have them with them upon this dangerous and hazardous undertaking.

The *Valhalla* first touched at Greenland, in order to take on more men and supplies, then plowed westward and southward, and finally the cry of "Land! Land!" sounded from the bow, where stood a Viking peering keenly into the distance. As the ship neared the coast it could be seen that the shore was heavily wooded. Dense forests grew down to the gray rocks upon the wave-tossed beach, and, as they neared the coast, flocks of sea-gulls rose from the water and screamed at the mariners.

The *Valhalla* was anchored. Several of the sailors went ashore in a boat and wandered inland. Biarne, himself, was with the voyagers, and, as he walked up to a gushing brook, was much surprised to see a large, dark animal, with spreading antlers, go crashing off in the brush. It was a bull moose, but Biarne had never seen such a curious beast before, so he was much excited over the discovery.

The weather was magnificent, and, after the sailors had been on shore for two days, Captain Leif sent Biarne after them to tell them that he wished to cruise further southward. It took Biarne some time to find the Vikings, as they had wandered far inland, but eventually he managed to deliver his message.

All returned to the *Valhalla*. The great sail was hoisted, and, dipping the massive oars into the clear, blue water which lapped musically against the high sides of the ship, the prow was turned southward so that the Vikings could coast along the shore.

The wind was northwest. The sea was rolling high with white-capped breakers, and, soon sailing out of sight of the land, the *Valhalla* careened southward for two days. Then land was seen again, and Leif steered towards it.

The ship drew closer and closer to the land. Finally the anchor was lowered, and many went ashore, but, finding nothing of great importance, the Vikings returned to the *Valhalla*. She was steered along the coast and finally came to a place where a river emptied into the sea. The stream seemed to course through a large basin, or lake, which was teeming with all manner of fish.

"Rah!" said Leif the Lucky. "We will spend the winter here!"

Down went the anchor into the sandy bottom and the *Valhalla's* great square sail was lowered to the deck. She swung gracefully around until her bow pointed into the outgoing tide, and all gazed at the beautiful shore, where pine and hemlock trees grew close to the water's edge.

Biarne and Eric had been in one of the boats which had been used to tow the ship into the lake, for the outgoing tide was very swift. They now came back to the *Valhalla*, clambered aboard, and assisted the Vikings in loading their bedding and tents into the boats.

"I know that we shall have a glorious time in this new country," cried Eric, joyously.

CHAPTER IX
Vinland

"**Y**es, this is a good land to spend the winter in," said old Staumfroid. "The days are longer than in Greenland, and, because of the great quantities of salmon in the stream, we will not want for food."

"It is a good country, cried Volga, one of the sailors. "We will rest well throughout the winter months."

The tents were soon put up upon the beach. There was much dew upon the grass, and one of the Vikings lifted some of the water to his mouth.

"I swear, comrades," said he, "this dew is sweeter than any dew I ever tasted before. It is indeed a good country."

There is, in fact, a sort of "honey dew" to be found on the coast of New England, in America, which tastes very sweet, and this is what the Viking had lifted to his lips.

Leif Ericson now divided his crew into two divisions.

"We must explore the country," said he.

Biarne and Eric went with the party which Staumfroid was leading. As they journeyed inland, they found that the land which they had discovered was a rich and fertile one. The forests showed signs of game, and, also, of men; so it was plain that there were inhabitants in this new-found territory.

"Suppose we should run upon some of the people who dwell here," said Biarne, as they trudged along. "If they are a warlike race, we should fare ill."

"No danger!" answered Eric, smiling. believe that we could easily be a match them, for are we not Vikings?"

He looked very proud, as he said this, and Biarne could not help laughing at him.

Leif the Lucky's foster-father, named Tyrker, was in the party. Not long after this, he became separated from his companions, and apparently was lost in the woods. Leif, himself, was much worried over his disappearance.

"I fear me that my father will become much muddled in his mind as to our whereabouts," said he. "It is not good to be lost in a strange country where there are enemies about. Here, Eric! Here, Biarne, help me look for the old fellow!"

The boys hurried off into the woods, but did not go very far, as they, themselves, were in fear of being lost. Suddenly they heard Leif shouting, and, running back, found that his father had returned. The old gentleman seemed to be very much excited. He was grimacing and talking to himself in his own "south country "tongue.

"Pray be quiet, Father," said Leif. "What is it that disturbs you so?"

The old man looked at him with wide open eyes.

"I did not go very far, my son," said he. "Yet I found vines and grapes. Yes, as good vines as in our own land."

Leif smiled broadly.

"That is indeed good," said he. "This is certainly a fine land, if grapes are here, so that we can make the red wine. I shall have to call it Vinland."

"Well spoken," said Tyrker. "It is a splendid country and a fit place for our people to come to."

They all started back towards the beach where they had pitched their tents, seeing abundant signs of game on the way; and soon arrived at the curving shore of the river, where the *Valhalla* lay gracefully at her anchorage.

"Men," said Captain Leif the Lucky, "we shall now have two things to do. We shall gather grapes and shall fell trees, in order to load our ship with lumber. But we must prepare for the cruel winter and must build ourselves a log house. Come, bestir yourselves. Eric and Biarne, get the axes ready and we will quickly go after the trees in the neighborhood, so that, when the cutting north wind blows, we shall have no cause for distress and suffering."

The boys paddled out to the *Valhalla*, found the axes, and returned to the land. Soon the chips were flying, the trees were falling, and the foundations of a large house were laid.

"Aren't you glad that you came along?" said Biarne to Eric, as they toiled over the timber cutting. "This promises to be a place where we can surely spend a pleasant winter."

"Indeed I am," said he. "We can have fine fishing in the bay, and we can go after deer and those big brown animals with spreading antlers which live in the deep woods."

The Vikings, in fact, had already caught many fine fish, which swam in the depths of the round basin, through which the blue and rippling waters of the river coursed into the sea. They were particularly pleased with the vast quantities of salmon which swam in the stream. They caught many of them; so many, in fact, that they grew tired of eating their flesh and longed for some other kind of diet. The log house progressed rapidly and it was not long before a magnificent structure stood upon the shore.

Was not this captain well named when they called him Leif the Lucky? He was the first man to find the great Western world, in spite of the fact that Christopher Columbus is supposed to be the first European to have ever visited America. None of the wise men of Europe had ever dreamed that there was a vast Continent far to the west of them, and was it not wonderful luck that Leif had discovered this country? Leif, himself, did not understand his own good fortune nor did he realize what he had found. "It is a good place," said he. "And we shall take a boatload of grapes and timber back with us to Greenland."

Eric and Biarne were assisting the sailors in the completion of their house when Leif strode up.

"We shall have a good winter here, boys," he said; "but I

fear greatly that we shall be attacked by some of the people who live in this country."

Just then a loud and peculiar call echoed from the dense forest, and an arrow whizzed by the ear of the staunch Viking leader.

CHAPTER X

The Battle with the Skrellings

Leif Ericson was a large man, but he was as agile as could be. Dodging the whizzing shaft, he ran quickly to the new-made house and there seized his own bow and arrow, his spear and his breast-plate.

"Come, my Vikings!" he cried. "I f these natives intend to drive us from the land, let us make it well worth their while."

"Hurrah!" shouted his followers, as they, too, ran to seize their bows, their arrows, and their spears. "We will show these Skrellings that the Vikings are not easily frightened."

A shower of darts and arrows was coming from the woods, as the Norsemen made ready to defend themselves. A series of shrill and startling cries rose from the timber; but, although an occasional arrow whizzed through the air from the direction of the dense forest, no heads of the enemy were exposed, and it was impossible to guess what was the size of the attacking party.

Biarne was at first quite frightened; but when he saw the unconcern with which Leif took the whole affair, he regained his composure. Strapping around his body one of the many breastplates which the Vikings had brought with them, he took up a bow and arrow and stood near the gallant Leif, who seemed not at all afraid of the yelping natives, whose war-like cries echoed from the dense underbrush.

The Vikings now ranged themselves in battle array and prepared to defend themselves, should the Skrellings, or natives of Vinland, debouch from the bush and make an onrush upon them. But no attack came. Instead, while the wild war-whoops continued, and an occasional arrow issued from the forest, the natives seemed to have no intention of issuing forth to engage in a hand-to-hand encounter.

"Let us advance into the woods," said Leif, at this juncture, "and show our yelping foes that the Vikings are men of red blood. Come, Norsemen, to the attack!"

Suiting the action to the words the brave Norse adventurer started for the woods, and, penetrating into the glade, drew his bow and shot an arrow at the head of one of the Skrellings, which he saw just above the side of a giant log. He missed the object of his attack by full a yard.

The rest of the Vikings now burst into the woods with a wild "hullo," and were met with a shower of arrows. Nothing daunted, they rushed forward and quickly routed the enemy from their hiding-places.

And what manner of men were these Skrellings? They were sometimes called Smaellingar, or small men. The red Indians did not then inhabit the coast of America, and these white people, small and squat in stature, but with heavy hair upon their bodies, were the owners of the land. The Indians said that the Great Spirit gave them the country after he had wrested it from the Skrellings.

They were a warlike race, and fought with spears, with bows and arrows, and with stone axes. They had skin boats, whereas the red Indians who followed them, used birch-bark canoes, or boats fashioned out of logs. They wore armor of deer and moose skin, and had shields fashioned from the same material.

The Skrellings held their ground only for a few moments. Apparently they had no relish for a hand-to-hand encounter with their giant invaders, who had on such curious-looking things that made their arrows bounce away when they struck them. So, after a terrific yelping, they turned and ran pell-mell into the forest, followed by the spears and arrows of the Vikings. Not a single Norseman had been dangerously wounded, although many of them had been struck by the flint-leaded arrows of the Skrellings; several, indeed, had been pierced through the thighs and calves of their legs; but, as the arrows were not poisoned, they did not seem to mind the injury.

The Vikings had been more accurate in their aim. The bodies of two of the Skrellings lay pierced by many arrows. As the Norsemen gazed upon these curious men of the new country, they found them to be swarthy and sinewy creatures with hairy faces and long black locks. They seemed, also, to be well fed and fairly well clothed, although the heavy skins, which they wore, had been unable to keep the arrows which

PICKED UP A ROUND SHIELD OF THICK SKIN.

the Vikings had shot from penetrating to their bodies and dealing them a death blow.

"See, Biarne," said Eric, as he gazed upon the countenance of one of the dead Skrellings, "these fellows not only had on good clothing, but they also had splendid shields."

He reached over, as he spoke, and picked up a round shield of thick skin, upon which was painted the body of a beaver.

"And they belonged to the tribe of men, no doubt," answered Biarne, "who worshiped this animal with a thick tail."

"It certainly is a curious-looking beast," said Eric. "I never saw anything like this in either Greenland or Iceland."

But the boys were to see plenty of beaver in Vinland before they went home to their far distant land in the north Atlantic Ocean.

Leif Ericson seemed to be well pleased with the turn which the fight had taken.

"These Skrellings," said he, "will not attack us again in a hurry. We have given them a good drubbing and they have learned what it is to attempt to frighten the Vikings. I'll warrant that we will have little more trouble with them in the future. Come, boys, back to our camp and catch some salmon for our supper."

All now returned to the beach, and, while some resumed work on the house, others jumped into the boats, paddled down the stream, and, with fish-hooks and lines, attempted to catch fish for the evening meal. The smoke ascended from the fires upon the shore: the axes and hammers rang; and the

Vikings made this once dull place look animated, indeed. The fight was soon forgotten; the Skrellings, in fact, seemed to have retired far inland, where, no doubt, lay their camp, or their houses. At any rate no fierce war-whoops came from the dense woodland; instead, the beautiful notes of a wood-thrush echoed tunefully from the somber pines and hemlocks, sounding as if some organ were being piped by the talented and invisible hands of a true musician.

CHAPTER XI

The Pirate Ship

"**B**iarne!"

"What is it, Eric?"

"There is trouble in the wind!"

"Eh! What!"

"Yes, trouble, I say; much trouble, for the ravens have been croaking, and there is a strange sound from out the mist."

A thick fog lay over the winding river which coursed through the lake into the sea, and rolled across the marshes upon its border. It enveloped the *Valhalla* as she swung gracefully at anchor, and it hid from view the great log house, which Leif and his men had constructed upon the shore.

Biarne listened, and, sure enough, away down at the mouth of the lake, where it emptied into the sea, could be heard a muffled noise.

"What do you suppose it is, Eric?" said he.

"A bittern, perhaps!"

"It's too loud for that!"

"A flock of geese!"

"Oh, no, they are far north upon their breeding grounds and have not yet flown southward."

"Then, what?"

As Biarne spoke, the sun began to burn off the fog and great rifts commenced to appear in the bank of mist. Finally the far distant shore of the bay was visible, and, peering intently into the distance, the two young Vikings saw a strange and astonishing sight. Another Viking ship—in fact, the very counterpart of the *Valhalla*—with gleaming oars and large, square sail, lay at the end of that inland sea. What a thrill it sent through the two young adventurers.

But the ship had been seen by others. There was a wonderful bustle and confusion near the camp of the Norsemen; there was a dashing and running about; a seizing of weapons; a curious peering into the far distance, where the strange visitor lay ominously near the stronghold of these sturdy adventurers. Captain Leif made haste to put on his armor.

"My Vikings," said he, "we will soon have a more desperate affair than that fracas with the Skrellings."

Drifting slowly along in the slight southerly breeze lay the stranger; dark in hull, ominously menacing, her sail flapping wearily, her great curving prow cutting the blue water with a ribbon of white. With the wisps of vapor eddying around her in the gentle southerly breeze, she looked like a grim phantom, hovering near, with the black hand of death at the helm.

The Vikings were soon prepared for battle. Quickly incasing themselves in their breast-plates, and seizing their shields, bows, and spears, they crowded to the boats and were paddled to the sides of the *Valhalla*. The anchor was hauled from the sandy bottom, the sail was run aloft, and, dipping the long oars into the brine, the great ship bore down upon the stranger, which still lay there, drifting, idling along, as if prepared for any encounter.

"Look well to your slings and arrows, my friends," shouted Leif, as he firmly seized the helm. "We will find a foe, here, well worthy of our steel, I'll warrant."

"That's the truth," spoke Eric, as he buckled on his breast-plate. "She looks to me like a pirate ship."

"And will she stand?" asked Biarne, curiously.

"That she will," answered a grizzled Viking, as he affectionately ran his fingers down his sword blade. "She will stand, for you notice that her crew are making no effort to paddle her to the harbor's mouth."

On, on forged the *Valhalla*, and still the stranger did not attempt to escape. On, on sped the Norsemen under Captain Leif, until they drew so close to the great, brown hulk in the offing that they could see the oarsmen on the deck.

As the Vikings eagerly peered at the visitors they saw brown, sunburnt and tawny-bearded faces beneath high caps of steel. Breast-plates flashed and glistened in the sun, spears reared their pointed heads from behind the high gun-whales. The visitors were apparently from the coast of France, or perhaps from the land lying upon the German Ocean. They rolled out a fierce song of war and shook their fists vindictively at the oncomers.

"It will be a battle royal," said Biarne.

Crash!

An arrow whizzed from some sturdy hand upon the deck of the newcomer, and a sharp barb flew by Biarne's ear, only to bury itself in the stout, oak planking near the mast.

Leif had been in many a fierce battle before and he stood at the helm with perfect calmness, directing his men with the ease and confidence of a veteran.

"Bear in close," he cried to those at the starboard oars. "Back water," to those on the port side. "We will reach the side of yonder pirate and have hand-to-hand fighting at once. It is the only way to handle these men of iron."

The *Valhalla* sheered off sideways, and bore down, steadily yet swiftly, upon the stranger. Her sail was flapping as she sped along, and, although the sail of the visitor had filled away, her helmsman bore up into the wind, so that she was bow on. Leif had steered in many another such encounter. He gently played with the rudder, and, as the *Valhalla* sped onwards, suddenly turned her bow so that she ranged along the side of their opponent. In a moment the grappling hooks sped through the air and the two sea warriors were linked together in the grip of death.

It did not take long for the Vikings to clamber over the rail and meet the foe in hand-to-hand battle. The arrows flew, axes crashed against steel and iron, blows rang upon cuirass and helmet, groans and sharp cries of battle sounded above the grinding of wood as the two great hulks rubbed against each other.

The strangers were a fierce and warlike crew. They fought well.

"Men, either you must conquer," cried Leif, "or we must all leave our bones in Vinland."

But the enemy were no match for the Norsemen. Several of the latter had already fallen, it is true, for the strangers shot accurately with their bows and struck out right valiantly with sword and with battle-axe. In spite of this, the Vikings drove them back to the stern of the ship, where, holding their shields before them, they ranged themselves in a circle, back-to-back, determined to battle until the last gasp.

Leif, himself, now took part in the fray. Leaving the helm in the charge of Thorwald, he leaped across the gunwale, and, with ax in hand, rushed into the thick of the fight. It was not long before the circle of steel had been broken, before these valiant invaders had been all either killed or disarmed, and the wild songs of the Vikings sounded shrill and clear above the groans of the wounded and dying. The Norsemen had conquered.

CHAPTER XII
Buried Treasure

"And, who are these warlike strangers?"

Eric, who had spoken, with head bruised and battered from a sword-thrust, was peering into the hold of the conquered ship.

"At least they did not run away?" said Biarne. "I believe that they are pirates." "Pirates?"

"Yes, even as we might become if we had to. These fellows have been preying on their weaker comrades on the sea."

The hold, in fact, was full of boxes, bales, and a valuable cargo of ivory. The strangers had either bartered with some natives upon the coast of Africa, or else had intercepted some vessel traveling overseas from the tropic land.

Leif Ericson had suffered no injury from the encounter. He was now seated near the center of the ship while his men held a few of the prisoners before him. He was questioning them as to their nationality, and their purpose in visiting this strange and unexplored country.

The strangers, it seems, were from the coast of Spain. Driven westward by a series of storms, they had fallen in with some traders from France; had captured them; had seized all of the most valuable part of their cargo; and had put all of their captives to death in order to avoid trouble of carrying them upon their own vessel. The treasure in the hold of the staunch craft was worth a large sum of money.

What would the Vikings do with it? Should it be divided, or should it go, for the most part, to Leif the Lucky?

Eric and Biarne were much interested in the inspection of the pirate ship, which was a trifle smaller than the *Valhalla*. Also, it was built of lighter timber, and had a great, high stern.

The deck was soon cleared of all signs of the recent affray, and the two boys aided in binding up the wounds of the prisoners. They were fierce-looking fellows, with tanned skins and great masses of coal black hair. They seemed to be resigned to their fate, and took matters with calmness.

Leif appeared to be much gratified at the result of his attack.

"Here," said he, "is a great treasure,—a fitting reward for all of our exertions. We are well repaid for our tremendous battling with this pirate crew. We will sail back to our mooring and to-morrow will decide what will be done with this valuable cargo."

The *Valhalla* had dropped astern, by now, and, with sail well filled, had started to return to her moorings in front of the place, on the beach, where the Vikings had built their house.

The sail was hoisted on the pirate ship and it was soon driven by the wind and oars towards the sandy shore. Leif and his men were certainly well pleased with their venture, and all sang lustily as the boat surged through the blue water. Finally they neared the *Valhalla*, which was at anchor; but, by Leif's orders, the bow of the pirate ship was driven on the beach.

"Now, lads," said the bold Viking to the two youngsters, "we will have to decide what is to be done with this treasure. It is more than I can claim for my own share, as all of my gallant men aided and assisted me in its capture."

"Yes," said Biarne, "but I feel sure that it will be safe here in Vinland, and that no one will touch it until we are ready to take it away."

No sooner had the pirate ship been beached, than she was securely fastened to the bank by means of long ropes. The Vikings sprang ashore, and were soon busily engaged in landing the jars of gold coin; the bales of valuable silk; and the numberless silver and jeweled ornaments which the pirates had captured from many a weak and unsuspecting crew. These were placed in a great pile and the Vikings gathered about their leader to hear what he had to say.

"My gallant Norsemen," cried Leif, "a portion of this treasure belongs to me, of course. The rest shall be divided amongst all of you. I feel that I should have at least a third; the remaining two-thirds should be apportioned amongst those who assisted in the taking of this vessel."

"That is fair," said old Thorwald, quite loudly.

"Yes, that is certainly fair," said Biarne also.

But a few of the Norsemen shook their heads.

"I put two of the pirates out of the way, bold Captain,"

said one stout fellow, called Huriulf, "certainly I should be entitled to more of the treasure than those who did little."

"Yes, and I, too, fought as hard as Huriulf," spoke another: Hake by name. "I should have a share proportionate to the work that I have done."

Thus dissention began.

Leif looked grave as he pondered over the matter. His followers stood around him in a half circle. They were a hardy-looking set, with their high helmets, their steel breast-plates and their long pikes in their hands.

"Well, my bold friends," said he, at length, "I cannot see that you should have more than the rest, but we will put it to the vote of all. What say you, men? Shall these two have more than the rest of you?"

"No! No!" came from all sides.

Leif smiled.

"You see, my lads," said he, "your friends and companions do not think that you should get what you wish."

The two Vikings looked sullen, but, as they made no remark, it was apparent that they were satisfied with the verdict which their mates had rendered.

The division of the treasure now went on. Leif Ericson, who had certainly been rightly christened "The Lucky," took one-third, as near as he could reckon. The rest was divided into equal portions, Eric and Biarne each receiving their proper share. But what was now to be done with the treasure?

THEY BURIED THEIR PORTIONS OF THE PIRATE GOLD.

"I'll tell you what I am going to do with my portion, Eric," said Biarne. "I am going to bury it."

"An excellent idea," answered Eric. "Where?"

"Up on the beach, up near those hemlock trees. No one will ever know it, if we put it there at night."

"You are right."

"We'll do it right away."

So, that very night Eric and Biarne carried their share of the treasure far up the beach, and, beneath a great rock where a single pine seemed to grow as a sentinel, they buried their portions of the pirate gold. They marked the rock with a cross and a number six, just opposite the spot where the treasure lay, and, trudging back to the hut, were soon fast asleep.

CHAPTER XIII

Winter in Vinland

The days now passed pleasantly enough, and, although the Vikings feared an attack by the Skrellings, none came. The great forest, back of their log house, stretched into the far distance a solid mass of waving green, from out which sounded the strange caterwaulings of the lynx, the drumming of the red-headed wood-pecker, or the deep grunting of a bull moose. As the fall advanced, there came a restful, quiet and beautiful season known as Indian summer, when a curious haze hung over the winding river, when sometimes scarce a ripple disturbed the surface of that curving stream which flowed through the inland lake into the sea; and when the dried and rustling leaves hung to the trees as if they were pieces of parchment.

Eric and Biarne often fished in the deep waters of the bay, to secure their share of the provisions for the winter which was approaching; and sometimes they chased the black ducks which settled upon the quiet water, on their journey from the far north to the warmer climate of the southern country. They likewise swam in the cold water, paddled far down to the harbor mouth, and explored the numerous islands which lay there, like sentinels watching the ever changing tides of this new-found river.

Then they joined the Vikings in their expeditions into the interior where were the vines which Leif's foster father had discovered. These were now hung with clusters of ripened grapes which were gathered into large bags and were carried to the huts upon the beach. Some of the Norsemen pressed out the juice and made a sweet wine from these purple berries which was much enjoyed by the daring sea voyagers. Traces of the Skrellings were often seen, but it was apparent that their first skirmish with the Norsemen had taught them a lesson, and that they did not care to meet again in battle.

The earth was tracked with the prints of deer and moose. Ruffed grouse, or partridges, often whirred away as the boys trudged through the forest, and, although they would try to shoot them with their arrows, it was very difficult to hit one unless it could be approached when in a tree. Sometimes the unsuspecting birds would sit peering down upon Eric and Biarne, as they walked through the forest, and were apparently so interested in these new kind of animals that they would remain there craning their necks until a stone-tipped arrow from an ashen bow would send them fluttering to the ground. They would be taken home and broiled over the fire for supper, and they were greatly relished by the Vikings, who grew rather tired of fish, and therefore were much pleased to get this addition to their larder.

"But, Eric," said Biarne, one day, "if we could only get a moose!"

"Wait until the winter sets in and the snow falls," said Eric. "I am sure that then we can track one of those monster deer through the forest and can catch him as he flounders through the snow."

"I believe that we can do so," answered Biarne. "It is growing very cold, now, and I feel that winter will soon be here."

The days were getting to be perceptibly shorter. By and by, as Eric lay dreamily gazing up at the stars, one evening the strange "honk! honk!" of a flock of geese sounded from the blue dome above his head. He purposely had stretched his bed outside the log hut in which he usually slept and the guttural notes made him start and sit up. Yes, winter was coming. The geese were flying southward, driven from their breeding grounds in far off Labrador by King Winter with his breath of ice and of snow.

Not long after this, the flakes began to fall, and, in order to keep the cold from the log houses, great roaring fires were built to warm them. The Vikings had been busy cutting wood, so that there was a plentiful supply on hand. This was piled behind their houses and all were quite ready for a hard and bleak winter season. The forest was apparently deserted by the Skrellings.

But there were other denizens of the woods.

One day, as Biarne was busily engaged in sharpening a

spear-point, he heard a long and mournful howling from the forest.

"Wolves!" said Eric, who was standing near him. "They say that they have grown very fierce from hunger."

Biarne crept nearer to the fire.

"I believe you," said he. "They must be big fellows, indeed. Certainly they make a mournful enough noise. I am almost frightened."

"Oh, that needn't frighten you," Eric answered. "Come, go with me to-morrow into the forest with old Staumfroid and we will see if we cannot track a moose."

"I would certainly enjoy that," said Biarne, laughing. "We will first make some snow-shoes, so that we can run over the crust."

This did not take very long to do. The Vikings had shot some deer, had dried the hides, and had made long strips of deer skin. With these the boys soon made broad-bodied snow-shoes which would easily hold them up upon the hard crust.

The next day, with old Staumfroid as their companion, they entered the forest and trudged back into the interior, past the wonderful vines of grapes which were now buried deep in a mantle of white. Occasionally they saw the V-shaped print of a deer's foot, where one had wandered through the wood, and occasionally, also, a print like the foot of a dog. A wolf had been by, and sad indeed would be the fate of any unsuspecting deer who would fall in the path of one of these scavengers of the forest.

At last old Staumfroid stopped and pointed at a big track in the snow.

"It is the monarch of the wood," said he. "Biarne, look at this!"

Biarne saw a big, broad foot-print like that of a great ox. A bull moose had passed by.

"Can we get him?" he asked eagerly.

"Yes," answered old Staumfroid, "if you follow my advice."

"What is that?"

"Keep doggedly to his trail! Never give up! He will run a long way, but we can tire him out as the snow is deep. When we get close to him, you must both run in on either side and shoot your arrows into his flanks, while I head him off and attempt to dispatch him with a spear."

"We will do as you say," said both the boys.

Now they settled down to work, and, gliding over the crust, were soon speeding upon the trail of the moose.

On, on they went through the forest, and fresher, ever fresher, became the tracks of the huge animal. On, on, they continued, and finally they saw a great brown mass ahead of them. It was the bull, who, terrified at their approach, was plunging through the deep crust in a desperate effort to escape.

"Now hurry, boys," cried old Staumfroid. "I will head him off."

Suiting the action to the words the Norseman ran swiftly ahead, spear in hand, and, as the bull stopped and glared at him with blood-shot eyes, he hurled his spear at him and struck him full between the antlers.

Meanwhile Biarne and Eric had shot their arrows into his flanks. With a great grunt of pain, the huge animal fell over on his side, while his blood crimsoned the crystal snow.

"Hurrah!" shouted the boys. "Hurrah!"

"Now, boys, we'll take the haunch of the old fellow home, but we must hang up the head and antlers so that the wolves cannot get them."

With his long knife old Staumfroid soon had the haunch cut away, the head was severed from the body and placed far up in the branches of a tree, and, swinging the meat upon his back, the Viking turned his face toward the huts upon the beach.

The boys followed, but they were not alone. As they went forward, a noise made Biarne look behind him. There, in the black forest, were two huge, gray wolves. They snarled and showed their fangs.

In spite of this the boys went forward, But as they came to the cluster of cabins, the wolves were still on their trail. They stopped, howling dismally, as the old Viking, with his two companions, broke from the forest into the clearing where were their huts.

"My, but I'm glad that I am not out in the forest alone," said Biarne, while his teeth chattered.

CHAPTER XIV
The Plot

The winter was not as severe as Leif had expect d. The Vikings were all well and healthy. One thing alone marred the pleasure of their stay, and that was the fact that the pirates, whom they had captured, seemed to be very quarrelsome, and it was difficult to keep them in order.

Eric was growing in strength and in vigor, but he was looking forward to the spring sea-son, when it would be possible for them to hoist the sails on both the *Valhalla* and the pirate ship and coast back to Greenland and Norway. Biarne, too, looked forward to the time when they could all be off again.

But exciting events were to occur, for dissentions had already arisen over the treasure which had been captured from the pirates.

Late, one afternoon, Eric had left the hut and wandered down the beach for quite a distance. He was looking at a reddish glow in the sky and wondering how far away the great North Pole might be, when he heard two voices in earnest conversation.

Carefully stealing up the beach, he hid himself behind

a rock and saw that the voices were those of a sailor called Haldor and a man named Avalldania. Haldor, who had a red beard, and a scar on his forehead, was speaking quite loudly.

"I know," said he, "that those two boys have hidden their part of the treasure, and in a place not so far away. You and I must search the beach, comrade, and I am sure that we can find where it lies buried."

"How do you know this?" asked the second.

"Why, man, I have looked into all their belongings, when they have been off hunting in the woods, and I have found nothing of the treasure. Where, then, have they placed it?"

Eric's heart began to beat loudly against his ribs. So their prized possessions had been searched, had they? This was why he had often found his bedding disarranged; some one had been looking for his share of the treasure. He was glad, very glad, that he had buried it.

"I think that the place cannot be far away," continued Haldor. "We must search the beach well. Perhaps we can find some sign on a rock; some sign which will tell us where we can unearth this gold."

Again Eric's heart pumped against his side. What if they were to run upon the cross which he and Biarne had made?

The voices now arose again.

"I'll tell you what, comrade," Haldor remarked, "we will not only look for this treasure, but we will gather other stout souls to our way of thinking; we will mutiny on the way home; and all the treasure will be ours before we reach the coast of Greenland."

"Comrade, will this be possible?"

Eric shuddered.

"Yes," replied Haldor, "and it will be a great thing for both of us. We will live in peace and comfort forever!"

"We will do it."

Eric crouched behind the rock, as he saw the burly forms of Haldor and Avalldania rise from the sandy beach. What if they should see him? He was breathless with excitement and fear.

But they did not see him. Instead of this they wandered along the beach, looking for something—Eric well knew what—and, when he saw them near the place where the treasure was buried, he watched them very eagerly indeed. They had keen eyes, but they were not keen enough to see the cross which Biarne had chiseled on the rock.

Eric watched closely, and when he saw that the two Vikings had gone safely by the place where the treasure lay hid, he turned and ran back to the hut.

"Biarne," he whispered, when he had found his comrade nestled down in his sleeping bag. "Biarne, I have bad news to tell you."

"What can it be, Eric? Your face seems to be very red."

"Yes, there are persons looking for our treasure. And a plot to mutiny is on foot."

"To mutiny?"

"Yes, and to steal all of the treasure on the return trip home."

"You must tell Captain Leif, at once."

"Would you?"

"No, stay! I would not tell him now. We will wait until the danger threatens, and then we will warn him so that he will be well prepared."

"That is sensible advice. I will do as you say."

"Leif will be quite ready for these fellows and I'll warrant that they will rue the day that they ever attempted to mutiny against our captain."

As he ceased speaking Leif, himself, entered the room, rosy with health, his flaxen locks streaming over his shoulders. Such a picture of manly strength and vigor the boys had never seen before.

"Well, boys," said he, "the spring is here."

"We must soon bid good-by to Vinland. And very sorry I'll be to go, for we have had a merry time of it."

"You are right, good Captain," said Eric. "We shall bring good news to our friends in Greenland."

"Good and great news," Leif answered. "News of a new country with grapes, wild savage inhabitants, and glorious salmon in the streams. I'll warrant that it will not be long before other Vikings hasten to plant homes in beautiful Vinland."

CHAPTER XV

The Journey Up the River

"**B**iarne, let us build a canoe!"

Eric had been lying upon some skins in a corner of the hut, dreamily gazing at the ceiling, when the idea suddenly came to him that it would be a splendid opportunity to explore the curving river which ebbed and flowed before their hut. The winter had been a severe one, but it had now almost gone, and the little catkins upon the pussy willows warned them that the spring was near at hand.

"All right, Eric," Biarne answered. "We will strip some of the birch trees, from the forest, and will get old Staumfroid to show us how to make the frame to stretch the bark on. Then we will melt some pitch in order to caulk the seams, so that the water will not get inside, and will also fashion some paddles from pine wood."

It did not take long to get the bark. After this had been peeled away, old Staumfroid showed the boys how to make the frame-work. They labored for two weeks, and, at the end of that time, had fashioned a beautiful little canoe.

Carrying it down to the shore upon their shoulders, they

launched their craft upon the waters of the river; then they made the paddles and were all ready for the expedition.

"I think that we should not go too far," said Biarne, as he tried his paddle in the water. "For the Skrellings may be camped up the stream, and I would certainly not like to get into a fight with them."

Eric was quite thoughtful.

"You are quite right," said he. "Although we have seen nothing of them here, there may be plenty of them up the stream. We must take a great quantity of arrows, at any rate, for we may see a moose in the water." Old Staumfroid chuckled.

"I don't believe that you will see any moose at this season," said he.

As he spoke, Eric noticed that he held in his hand a piece of birch-bark upon which he had been writing, and this excited his curiosity.

"What have you been writing?" he asked.

Old Staumfroid smiled. "Boys," he said, "I have been writing a poem, a song of the Vikings. Do you want to hear it?"

"Yes! Yes!" cried both the boys. "Do read it to us, Staumfroid."

The old fellow was delighted at the interest which they showed in his work. So, clearing his throat, he read what he had written, in loud, clear tones.

"The wind is blowing from off the shore,
And our sail has felt its force,
For our bark bounds o'er the crested wave,
Like a wild and restive horse.
Our sharp prow cleaves the billows,
And breaks them into spray,
And they blithely gleam in the sunlight,
As we speed upon our way.

"To our oars we bend with a right good will,
And sorrows leave behind.
Like the white-winged gulls that around us
wheel,
We are racing with the wind.
Each day we'll pray to heaven,
Nor shall we pray in vain,
For the gods will watch o'er our steady barks,
And will guide us home again.

"Lord of the waves we are,
Kings of the seething foam,
Warriors bold from the Norseland cold,
Far o'er the sea we roam."

The boys clapped their hands.

"Why, that's fine," said Biarne, laughing. "You certainly know how to write poetry, Staumfroid. I thought that you were only a hunter."

Old Staumfroid chuckled. "Why, boys," said he, "I can write all kinds of good and beautiful things. When you get back from your trip I may have something else for you to hear."

The boys smiled.

"Why, that would be fine," they said in unison.

Now they filled the canoe with what supplies they needed for a few days, and, taking their bows, their spears, and plenty of arrows, they clambered in, and started up the winding river which was afterwards to be known as the river Charles. Waving good-by to the Norsemen, who had gathered on the bank to bid them adieu, they had soon paddled around the bend, and were speeding up the curving stream.

On, on, they went, marveling at the beauty of the country, the wonderful green of the trees, which were just coming into leaf, and the variegated flowers along the bank. They heard the song-sparrows singing in the bushes where the fresh green of spring made a beautiful back-ground for their speckled breasts. They heard the frogs piping in the meadows; the cawing of the crows; and the trill of the little red-capped chipping sparrows.

On, on they paddled, drinking in the clear air, and reveling in the beauty of the landscape. The river twisted and turned in great curves; and, save for the prints of deer in the banks, there was no sign of animate life.

Suddenly they turned a bend and almost ran against the body of a cow moose. She had immersed herself in the water, probably to get away from the flies, and, as the canoe shot close to her, she stumbled up on the bank with a great, bellowing grunt.

Eric was in the stern of the canoe, and sent it ahead with such a shove that it nearly struck the cow as she clambered up on the bank. Biarne slapped her on the tail with his paddle, and she went lumbering away as if stung by a giant hornet. The boys could not help laughing.

They kept on up the stream, the river twisting and turning in graceful curves. As they rounded a great bend, they saw before them the marks of men's footprints in the sandy soil.

"The Skrellings have been here," said Biarne, pointing to the footprints. "We must look out."

A place where the bushes had been torn up, on the bank, the marks of a fire and other prints left by men, showed the boys that certainly a camp of Skrellings had been there. The boys became cautious, and paddled more slowly up the stream.

When night came, they drew their canoe upon the bank, spread their robes beneath it, upon a bed of new-cut hemlock boughs, and, after broiling a fish for their dinner, lay down to rest. They were still half awake when a somber voice in the forest made them both sit up.

"Hoo-hoo-hoo, Hoo-hoo-hoo-hoot!" came from the blackness.

"My, do you suppose that is one of the Skrellings?" whispered Biarne.

No!" Eric answered. "It's a big, brown owl."

"Are you sure?"

"Certainly!"

Biarne seemed to be relieved.

"I'm glad to hear it," said he, "for I feared that it was one of the Skrellings giving notice of our whereabouts."

Again came the call, but, in a few moments the hooting seemed to be far away. The owl had moved.

"Hoo-hoo-hoo, Hoo-hoo-hoo-hoot!" came from the far distance.

At this, both of the boys breathed more easily and composed themselves in slumber.

CHAPTER XVI

The Fate of the Treasure

As the bright sun came over the hemlock trees, in the early morning, Eric and Biarne sprang up and joyfully prepared their breakfast.

"We will go a few more miles up the river and then will return home," said Eric.

Just as they were about to push off the canoe, something made Eric look down at the sandy soil, and what he saw there made him start backward. There were the prints of a man's naked foot.

"Biarne!" said he in a startled manner. "Yes."

"Look there!"

Biarne's eyes grew as big as two saucers. Could it be one of the Skrellings, he thought. They must be careful.

"Eric, we must start down stream immediately."

"You are quite right, Biarne. Here, help me shove the canoe into the water!"

The canoe was soon lifted from the shore and floated upon the surface of the river. Both boys clambered aboard, after hastily putting in their belongings. Then the bow was turned down stream, the paddles were seized, and they started away at a rapid pace. As they turned a bend, a fierce cry sounded from the bank and they knew that the Skrellings had seen them.

"Paddle, oh, paddle!" cried Biarne. "I am afraid that they will head us off, for it is very shallow here."

Eric said nothing, but dug his paddle into the water with a right good will and the boat fairly flew along. Again sounded the cry, and, as the boys swung the canoe around a bend in the stream, an arrow whizzed by the ear of poor Biarne, whose hair was fairly standing up from his head.

On, on paddled the boys, startling a great blue heron which flapped away, squawking dismally, and almost running into a flock of black ducks, which had alighted on the peaceful river on their way to the North. On, on they went, and farther and farther behind them echoed that warlike cry. They did not dare look behind them, but kept on manfully, while the perspiration ran down their brows.

At length they turned a great bend hi the river and Eric took in his paddle.

"Goodness, Biarne, but that was a tight squeeze," he said. "I believe that if we had not shoved off when we did we would have been captured by the Skrellings, for they must have been all around us."

Biarne looked furtively over his shoulder.

"You are quite right, Eric," said he. "We had a very narrow escape. But, after all, I do not believe that the Skrellings are such bad people. They might have treated us very well, indeed."

Eric laughed.

"Certainly what I saw of them hi the woods did not give me too high an opinion of them," he answered. "They looked to me like wild men."

The boys now chattered and laughed quite happily, for they felt that the danger was over. A bobolink rose from the bushes and flooded the air with beautiful cascades of melody; the sun shone upon the rippling water with brilliancy, and, as they floated along by some high rushes, a red-winged blackbird sang "Congaree! Congaree!" All was peace and beauty along the lovely river.

Running the canoe into the bank, the boys went ashore and ate their luncheon. Little did they think that a great Norse town, called Norumbega, later would be built where they were seated. It was to have walled docks and wharves, a dam, a fishway, and miles of stone walls along the Charles River, below. Later a town called Watertown, was to come into being on this spot. As the boys lay idly upon the bank, they had not the slightest idea that many Norsemen, in after years, would have their homes here, and would interest themselves in fishing, in cutting wood, and in building houses for their friends and their kinsfolk.

"I heard Thorwald say that we would begin the journey to Greenland very shortly," said Eric, as he lay upon his back, idly gazing into the air. "We had better dig up our treasure, to-morrow, Biarne. What say you?"

"I certainly agree, Eric. We must get it stowed away in

WATCHED THEM, WITH ONE FOOT IN
THE AIR AND HEAD ERECT.

sacks, and, if any one asks us what it is, we will say that it is the result of our trapping expeditions with old Staumfroid."

"I hardly think that would fool them."

"Well, we must take our chances."

The noon-day rest was now over, so, again entering their canoe, the boys continued their journey down stream. They felt that there was now no danger from the Skrellings, so took things easily.

Floating along gently and quietly, they startled a great, red buck deer as he was drinking from the stream. The animal started to run, as they whirled by, but stopped for a moment and watched them, with one foot in the air and head erect.

"Doesn't he look like a statue?" said Eric.

Biarne laughed.

"Yes, I'd like to have a picture of him just as he is."

The buck seemed to blow out his breath as if whistling; then turned, and, with a few bounds, was off into the forest.

The boys paddled onwards, and, just as dusk was appearing, reached the neighborhood of the huts which Leif had erected. They could see the smoke ascending from the chimneys, and dark forms moving on the beach, so they knew that all was well with the Vikings. They neared the place where they had buried their treasure, and quite unconsciously, Eric cast his eye in that direction. Something in the look of the ground made him uneasy, so he paddled towards the spot. As he drew nearer, a cry of dismay issued from his lips.

"Biarne, paddle on quickly!" he cried.

Biarne drove his paddle into the water and the bow of the canoe fairly shot through the blue river until the bank was reached. As Eric leaped to the shore, a cry of anger and dismay came from his lips.

"Biarne! Oh, Biarne! The treasure is gone!"

Biarne was too stunned to answer. As he looked before him, two great holes were in the beach; stone, sand, and gravel was thrown up on every side. Their precious possessions had vanished. Only one thing remained. This was a stake driven in the ground upon which had been affixed a board. On this had been written with a burned stick the word: "Skrelling."

The two boys sat down upon the sand and sobbed bitterly. Their treasure, their wonderful treasure, which they had thought of so fondly, and so often, had been stolen.

But they had little time for reflection, as all were preparing for the return trip to Greenland.

CHAPTER XVII

Back to Greenland

Flood tide.

The great, ebbing, surging blue current of the river rolled onward past the log huts of Leif and his adventurers. Tortuous, twisting, singing, crooning, and sweeping great brown pieces of seaweed along in its mad flight, it passed by the spot where later would stand the home of Henry Wadsworth Longfellow, the inspired poet, the man of sweetness and benevolence. It eddied and gurgled beyond the green marshes which lay near the future habitation of James Russell Lowell, that mystical dreamer of beautiful dreams at Elmwood. It was now deserted and silent, save for the occasional splash of a leaping fish, but almost a thousand years later its surface was to be dotted with the shells of many crimson-shirted oarsmen, who were to find healthful exercise upon its fresh and gurgling surface, and recreation, after the hours of study in the halls of the college which would spring into being near its sloping banks.

A bustle and confusion was now upon the shore, for Leif Ericson had given orders to get everything ready for the return journey to Greenland. The gray geese had begun to fly north again; their V-shaped lines had gone "honking "over the green marshes which lay before the low huts of the Vikings; the white-throated sparrows were trilling in the bushes, now verdant with the first, young flush of spring, and the soft notes of the hermit thrush sounded from the silence of the forest.

Flood tide.

The *Valhalla* swung at her moorings; and beside her lay the great pirate ship, her high prow topped with a dragon's head, jutting far out from the blue water. The river was dotted with the boats and skiffs of the Vikings, as they carried their belongings to the vessels and made preparations to go back to far distant Greenland. The huts were being rapidly dismantled, and the woods echoed with the laughter and shouting of the Norsemen.

Biarne and Eric had assisted in loading the *Valhalla* with lumber and with dried grapes; they had also placed a considerable amount of timber in the hold of the pirate ship. During the winter they had helped to dry a great many fish, and these had been stowed away in the hold. They also had killed some deer, had dried their hides, and were taking these back to their friends and relatives as a proof of their skill with the bow and arrow.

At last all was ready; the treasure had been stowed away; and the oars were dipped into the waters of the blue river. Eric and Biarne had not mentioned what had happened to their own portion, for they hoped that they would discover the thieves on the return trip. The anchors were drawn from the muddy bottom, the square sails were hoisted aloft, and the prows of the two Viking ships were turned towards the rounded basin through which the river flowed into the sea.

Captain Leif stood at the helm of the *Valhalla*, while old Staumfroid was at the tiller of the captured ship. As the wind filled the fluttering sails of the two graceful ships, they careened over to leeward, and a wild "Huzzah "came from the throats of the oarsmen. Their oaken oars splashed in unison, the two vessels drew onward, and began to slip towards the far distant Atlantic.

Eric stood near his friend, Captain Leif, and, as the *Valhalla* dropped down the winding stream, he gazed back wistfully at the log huts which had served them as such comfortable homes during the winter. Although the Vikings had put out most of the fires, some one had left one burning in the larger hut, where a thin wisp of smoke curled from the chimney into the air. Not a sound came from the green forest, which stretched backward as far as the eye could see into the blue distance. Vinland was being left to the Skrellings, the moose, the beaver, and the bear.

Farewell to Vinland!

A towhee bunting trilled a matin song from the edge of the great abysmal forest, as the ships went gliding past; a song sparrow sent cascades of sweet melody into the clear air; a squirrel chattered and scolded at the staunch adventurers from his perch on a pine-tree, as the square sails slapped in the increasing wind.

Farewell to Vinland!

The waves now danced and played with a thousand white-caps around the ships of the Norsemen, as they left the river, and, propelled by strong arms and oaken oars, forged ahead into the open bay. As Eric looked sadly and sorrowfully behind him, a great blue heron rose from the marshes at the head of the beautiful stream, and, flying upward with grace and precision, seemed to beckon good-by to the venturesome mariners, with his great flapping wings. The roar of the surf now came to the ears of the lad, as he wistfully gazed astern at the fast disappearing shore, and the lapping waves seemed to speak in accents of sadness and regret, "Farewell to Vinland!"

CHAPTER XVIII

Mutiny

Fair winds were behind the two Viking ships, and it was not very long before they had drawn far away from the low-lying shores of Vinland. The rowers bent to the oars with a will, singing an old Norse song as they propelled the high-sided vessels towards the east. The boys stood in the stern of the *Valhalla*, and looked long and intently at the fast disappearing shore line.

"Biarne, we have had a good time in Vinland," said Eric. "But now it is all over."

"Yes, but when shall we warn Captain Leif of the mutiny that has been planned?"

"We will do that to-night."

When darkness had settled upon the blue Atlantic, and the boats were drowsing along under their spreading canvas, Eric crept to Leif's side.

"Sir," said he, "I have bad news to tell you."

"What is it, my son?"

"There is mutiny afloat. Biarne and I heard two of the sailors talking, Haldor and Avalldania, and they are preparing to kill you and your faithful followers, and take the whole treasure for themselves."

Leif started up from the cask upon which he had been sitting.

"Wh-a-a-t?"

"Yes, what I tell you is the truth."

"Thank you, boy, for your information. I will see that these fellows are checkmated in their wild design."

Eric went back to his place in the center of the ship, and, while there, saw Captain Leif call several of his Vikings to his side. They were soon engaged in earnest conversation, and it was evident that Leif intended to be quite ready for any show of force upon the side of the mutineers.

Biarne had kept his eyes wide open and he had carefully hidden himself near Avalldania in order to see if he could not overhear the plans for seizing the *Valhalla*. That night he saw the treacherous Viking in conversation with several other Norsemen, and, from the expression upon their faces, he knew that they had decided to make an attempt at capturing the vessel before many days were over.

What would be the outcome of the battle? Biarne saw that Avalldania had a good many upon his side, but he also knew that those who would rally to Leif's banner were more numerous than those whom Avalldania could claim. There could be but one ending to the affair: the mutineers would be vanquished. So little Biarne felt fairly easy in his mind. He had the greatest confidence in Captain Leif.

The two ships sped onward. The mutineers obeyed all orders that were given them and seemed to bear no outward malice towards Leif and those whom they knew to be true to him. Day after day the vessels rose and fell upon the long, surging billows, as they plowed their way towards Greenland, and day after day the hardy Vikings plied the long, oaken sweeps. At last they neared that island of the Far North, whence they had come. It was now or never with the mutineers.

Biarne saw Haldor and Avalldania conversing very earnestly with one another and over-heard the whispered remark: "At seven o'clock to-morrow morning!" He guessed that this was the time set for the attack.

So he went to Leif and gave him warning.

"I will be ready when the time comes," said the Viking, laughing softly. "Avalldania had better beware."

The next day was a foggy one, and great banks of mist blew over the gray, surging ocean. Biarne and Eric had placed their shields where they could be easily reached, and waited for whatever might transpire. Nothing occurred until well after the time set by the mutineers. Then Avalldania, a sailor named Huriulf, and Haldor were seen to walk towards the bow. In a second they snatched up their shields and drew their swords, while Avalldania gave a great shout of battle.

Captain Leif was standing near the tiller, but, quicker than I can tell you, he had seized his own weapon. The shout had startled all the crew, and, in a moment more, those who were true to the staunch Viking, had ranged themselves by his side. Biarne and Eric, too, were ready for the fray.

"What means this, men?" shouted Leif, above the splashing of the waves. "Do you intend to attack your leader?"

Avalldania's eyes fell before the keen glance of the mighty Norseman, and, as he saw the men who ranged themselves by his side, he became less anxious to attempt to gain the mastery by force. But he had thrown down the gauntlet. What would Leif do to him should he now declare a truce, after he had made every show of an attack? Prompted by this thought, he threw himself upon the captain.

Leif met him with a sword thrust, which the mutineer parried, and then closed with the great Viking.

"To the rescue, friends!" shouted Avalldania, at this juncture. "If you do not come to my assistance, it will be all over with me!"

But the mutineers, although previously full of fight, had lost all their fire. Although those who had conspired to mutiny had seized their shields and other weapons, they hung back and made no effort to advance. Meanwhile it fared badly with Avalldania.

As he grappled with Leif and attempted to pull a dagger from his own belt in order to plunge it into the back of the noble Viking, he was seized upon either side by two stalwart Norsemen, who soon threw him to the deck and pinned him down. In a moment, his arms had been bound with ropes, and he lay there, glaring furiously into the laughing faces of those men of iron.

Meanwhile his followers had thrown down their arms, and had shouted out that they had meant no harm by this display of force, and that they surrendered. The mutiny had been short lived, indeed, but it was to the information furnished by Eric and Biarne that Leif and his followers owed their lives.

"Thank you, my boys, for what you told me," said Captain Leif, holding out a hand to each of the lads. "Had it not been for the notice which you gave me of the mutineers, I fear that they would have had their own way, and we would all have been slaughtered. You are good boys."

Both Biarne and Eric felt very proud at such praise from the great Leif Ericson.

CHAPTER XIX
The Treasure Discovered

Next day Biarne's mind began to revolve about the treasure which they had lost, and, going up to Eric, he said:

"Let's go below and look around among the things stored there. Perhaps we can find some trace of the stolen treasure."

"Why, Biarne," Eric answered, "isn't it strange? I was thinking the same thing. Come on! Let's go below!"

The boys climbed down to the place where the Vikings had packed away most of their belongings, and, with keen eyes, began to look at everything which might possibly contain their lost treasure. They pried in between bales of furs, stacks of dried fish, and pieces of sawed lumber; but, for a long time, it was a pretty hollow search. Finally Biarne climbed up in the bow, where it was so dark that he could only just see; but, Eric, who was behind him, heard him whisper.

"Eric! Eric! Come here, for I believe that I have unearthed something which will be of interest to you."

Eric scrambled up to the place where Biarne was kneeling, and found him with his hand upon a bag of deer skin. "Feel that!" said he.

Eric put his hand down and clutched the bag. There was something hard beneath it which felt like large, golden coins.

"Can it be the treasure?" he whispered. "I think so."

"Hurray! Then we have it on board, just as I thought."

As he spoke, a shadow darkened the hold, and the boys saw Haldor peering in their direction. Both of them crouched down low, behind a bale of fox skins.

"Comrade," said Haldor, turning to a second Norseman who had come to his side, "I thought that I heard something stirring."

"Hist!" answered the other, a sailor named Thor. "We must be careful what we say. You remember that the treasure is there."

"Yes."

"And it is buried well beneath the fox skins and lumber?"

"Yes."

"And no one suspected it. No one saw you stow it away?"

"Yes, Tellfroid did."

"Did he suspect what it was?"

"He questioned me."

"What did you say?"

"I told him that we had put a rock in there for ballast."

"A sorry answer!"

Haldor winced. "I admit it."

"Well, I certainly heard a noise! Are there any rats aboard?"

"None that I know of."

"Well, perhaps it was that tame fox which Tellfroid brought with him. The beast is a nuisance!"

The boys could not help chuckling. Eric snickered so loudly that he thought they heard him.

Apparently satisfied that no one was there, the two Vikings withdrew, while the boys wriggled from their hiding place and finally climbed on deck. Both were smiling broadly, for they knew that they would secure what really belonged to them when they should reach home.

The two ships plunged onward, and, as the sinewy Vikings swung the great oaken oars through the water, they sang a wild song of the Norseland. They passed the shores of New-foundland, saw many whales spouting and playing in the water as they left that land of flat stones far behind, and then, as they plowed their way toward Greenland, great schools of porpoises jumped and frolicked around them.

A dense fog now encompassed the ships, and, for fully a day they plowed through a sheet of white mist, but, at last the sun burned through the fog bank and the ships sped onward towards their goal. The white gulls went careening by, the massive billows surged and tossed, but the brave ships plowed onward, until—in the far distance—a thin, bluish-brown line upon the horizon told them that they were nearing Greenland.

Both Eric and Biarne were delighted to think that they would soon be back in their old home and would see their parents again, for Leif had promised to send them home in the first ship that left Greenland for Norway. They stood in the bow eagerly gazing at the nearing shore, and, occasionally they would help one of the men with an oar.

As they stood thus, old Staumfroid came up behind them and laid a hand upon either shoulder.

"Boys!" said he, "are you glad to get back after all your many adventures in Vinland?"

"Yes," said Eric, smiling. "But, Staumfroid, we have something that we want to tell you.

"Go ahead, my son, what is it?"

"You remember the treasure that Captain Leif captured from the pirates?"

"I certainly do."

"You remember that we both received a certain part of it?"

"Yes, what did you young rascals do with it?"

"We buried it on the beach."

"Near the camp?"

"Yes, near the camp."

"Well! well!" Old Staumfroid grew interested.

"And it was stolen from us by some men on this very ship."

"W–h–a–a–t?"

"Yes, and it is now down below in some sacks. Will you help us get it back?"

"Why, certainly, I will, if you can prove that it is yours."

"That we can do quite easily."

"All right. I will help you do it when we get to land."

Soon the ships entered the harbor of Bratthalia, and their anchors were lowered in the quiet waters of the little bay.

All the townsfolk came out and shouted a welcome to them. They blew horns, waved banners, and cried out in loud tones: "Skoal to Leif Ericson! Skoal to Leif Ericson and his brave Vikings! Welcome home to Greenland!"

CHAPTER XX
And All Ended Happily

The Vikings scrambled ashore, and, forming in a procession, marched up the main street, to the blowing of trumpets, the clashing of cymbals, and the rolling of rude drums.

Then they were carried to the town hall upon the shoulders of the inhabitants of Bratthalia, where Leif Ericson, himself, mounted a high platform and delivered a speech. He closed his remarks with the words:

"We are glad to get home, I can assure you, O people of Greenland. We are glad to get home from Vinland, the land of the salmon, the moose, the beaver, and the wolf, which we have left safely in the hands of the Skrellings. We have brought you much lumber and many dried fish, as a token of our affection for you, and we trust that some of you will follow us in explorations to 'Vinland, the Beautiful.' "

The boys clapped their hands at these remarks, and then went to look for old Staumfroid, as the vessel was to be unloaded next day, and they wished to be where they could get their treasure as it was handed over the side.

"Boys, I will be with you to-morrow," said old Staumfroid, "and when the treasure comes over the rail, you will hear from me, I can assure you. Rest content! Those two villains, Haldor and Thor, will not get it away from you as long as my name is old Staumfroid."

The boys were much overjoyed to hear him talk in this manner, and, bright and early next morning, they were down at the shore, where the *Valhalla* had been run up against a dock, and where the Norsemen were already at work in unloading her. Old Staumfroid was there, also, with a keen look in his eye.

Haldor and Thor mingled with the other men, and, after much lumber had been taken from the hold, they began to take out a quantity of skin bags which seemed to be very heavy, indeed. They were carried up on the beach and were placed next to some fox skins. When all had been removed from the hold, old Staumfroid walked over to the place where the bags lay, followed by Eric and Biarne. Leaning over, he felt one with his hand.

"What have we here?" said he.

Haldor was standing nearby and his face grew crimson. The scar upon his forehead took on a purplish hue.

"Ballast!" he muttered.

"Oh, no, my fine friend," said old Staumfroid. "This is not ballast. This is something else, I can assure you." Then he straightened up, "This is treasure which belongs to Biarne and Eric, and you dug it up upon the beach at Vinland."

The expression upon Haldor's face was anything but pleasant.

"It's a falsehood!"

In answer old Staumfroid took out his long knife and ripped a bag open. A quantity of golden coins jingled out upon the stones.

"What say you to that, sir?" he asked.

The thieving Norseman stood with his mouth wide open.

"Now, know you," continued Staumfroid, "that this treasure belongs to these two boys and I insist that it shall be returned to them. You dug it up on the beach in Vinland, and you must give it back to the rightful owners. If you do not do this, I will take the matter up before Leif Ericson, himself, and it will go hard with you."

Both Haldor and Thor looked at Staumfroid and walked away. Old Staumfroid smiled.

"Now, boys, this shall be taken to a safe place and you will both be rich young men," said he.

Not long afterwards, with the assistance of Leif Ericson, the boys sailed with their treasure for Norway. Long life and prosperity were to be their lot; but they often thought of their wonderful expedition to Vinland, the Beautiful. As the old Nornir had said, one with a red beard and a scar upon his forehead was to prove to be an enemy, but, thanks to old Staumfroid, all had ended auspiciously. The young Vikings lived happily ever afterwards, admired and respected by all the brave and daring Norsemen.

But what of Vinland?

Many other Norsemen, principal among whom was Thorfinn Karlsefni in 1007 A. D., sailed across the great, surging Atlantic Ocean to get fish and lumber in the new country. A settlement, called Norumbega, was made upon the Charles River, that river, filled with salmon, which flowed through a lake into the sea. But eventually this was deserted by the bold Vikings, who returned to their homes in Greenland, Iceland, and Norway; leaving high stone walls, artificial canals, and docks and wharves, to show where they had once lived in peace and comfort in beautiful Vinland.

THE END.